CW01044372

Finding Fleur

STARGAZING SERIES, BOOK TEN

D J COOK

Collaboration Organiser: Phoenix Book Promo
Editor: Heather Ross
Cover design and interior graphics: Shower Of Schmidt Designs
Formatting: Phoenix Book Promo
Starsign Credit: The Zodiac City

Scorpio

She does a lot for others because she's naturally caring.

With her, it's all or nothing, so she will not tolerate someone wasting her time (especially in relationships)

She loves hard but has no problem loving from a distance.

She's driven and powerful. She may test your loyalty. Once you cross her, she never looks at you the same.

She notices everything.

Finding Fleur Synopsis

Finding Fleur is book #10 of the Stargazing Series, a 12-book series of standalones.

Fleur Jansen dreams of travelling the world.
Even as a child, she rolled around in her grandparents' flower fields and watched the clouds enviously as they travelled all the places she wanted to go—free and without restraint.
Now a successful solicitor and with another promotion on the horizon, life is full of barriers stopping Fleur from fulfilling her dreams.
Fleur finally sees she's been living a nightmare and sets out on an adventure, with her travel journal and itinerary in hand.
That is, until her dreams fade to black.
Until disaster strikes.

Until all Fleur knows is broken.

Will she continue to chase down her dreams?

Will love and friendship prosper or will Fleur accept that dreams are just that, and reality can never live up to them?

Prologue

I wasn't the type of person to get nervous. Not normally. I'd stood up and presented many times in front of hundreds of people at confer-ences, and I regularly had to stand up in court to protect the integrity of my clients, but those nerves couldn't compare to how I felt going on a date with the man of my dreams.

I'd spoken to him for over two months online, but we'd never had a chance to meet. Was it that we were both so busy with work, or that we both kept creating excuses to postpone the possibility of being disappointed? We were so good from a distance.

I'd fawned over him for far too long not to be nervous.

I was worried that the past two months of excitement, a flame ready to burn as bright as they do on bonfire night, would instead be fighting for oxygen. I was worried the past two months would have been for nothing, because that's how it had always been. However, it did tell me something. It told me I was all in.

My office blocked the moonlight, casting shadows on the street as it towered above me. If I'd had my pass to get me in the building, I might have been persuaded to pay my desk a visit in order to give next week's cases a once over. I shook off that thought and refocused because the evening wasn't about my job. It was about me for a change.

I trailed along the cobbled streets I walked frequently, but this time was different. I hadn't walked in the centre of London in the black of night for a long time. The men surrounding me wore light polos and shorts instead of business suits. The women sported dresses that barely hung off their shoulders instead of blouses and jackets. The smell of alcohol was more pungent than usual, pouring from the people who swarmed around me rather than out of the bars that lined the streets.

I approached an arched doorway made of stone and stopped in my tracks, catching a glimpse of my reflection in an outdoor mirror in a beer garden. Nerves had taken over my body, my limbs still, my face panicked.

I wasn't worried about not liking him. He was attractive in his pictures: light stubble was present on his sun-kissed face, his hair a mixture of light and dark browns, and his lips—a delicate pink that I'd already pictured kissing far too many times. It wasn't his looks that stood out, though; it was his personality. Over the two months we'd spoken, it had been all about me. I couldn't wait to get to know him more, but my legs wouldn't move, frozen in fright that he'd look at me and not feel the same way I felt for him.

I pulled my shoulders high as I straightened my back, ridding the thought from my mind. A negative attitude wasn't how I'd been promoted from assistant solicitor to senior solicitor. It had taken hard work, dedication and countless nights without sleep. My career had always come first; I barely made time for the few friends I had.

I stepped towards the bar with a glass or two of wine acting as Dutch courage in my stomach, smiling at the bouncers flirtatiously before I entered the building. I ordered a drink, feigning elegance without glancing behind me, attempting to look like I didn't care whether Connor came.

"Fleur, is that you?" A familiar voice caressed me, one I'd heard on the phone many times but sounded even more gritty and delicious in person.

I turned slowly, my brown hair covering part of my flushed face, as I prepared myself for something to go wrong. It had to.

"Woah, you look... incredible." Connor caught his words as I smiled, turning my head and leaning inwards for a kiss on the cheek.

I looked him up and down slowly, allowing him to see me take him all in. His navy suit clung to him in all the right places, brought to life by a crisp white shirt, the cuffs showing perfectly at his wrists. He could have been wearing anything at all and he'd still have looked unreal. He could have said anything and his voice would have made the words taste sweet. He oozed swag, but didn't necessarily know the power he already held over me.

"I could say the same about you. I can't believe it's taken two whole months for us to finally meet." I couldn't help but grin.

"I know. It's you and your super official job,

speaking of which, did you get the promotion?" His gaze didn't leave mine. I struggled to find words to respond as I lost myself in him.

"Um... I did. You're now looking at an associate solicitor of Howarth and Co."

The promotion hadn't come as much of a shock. I'd been at the firm for a good few years and had made my mark winning some high profile cases, but nothing like the one I'd won the previous week, worth over eight million pounds.

"That's incredible!" His arms wrapped around me and the musk of his aftershave clung to my nose. "I guess drinks are on me then."

His fingers interlocked with mine, his thumb grazing my hand as he led me to our table. Strings of lights hung above us, illuminating the room and everything in it. Maybe it was my senses that were heightened, but I hadn't seen flowers and greenery as bright as that in a long time. I hadn't felt a touch as electric as Connors as we sat down and he placed his hand on mine.

"It's so good to finally see you. You have no idea how much I've been looking forward to this," he said, still connected to me physically, along with his gaze that wouldn't tear away from mine.

"Me too. So, you know about my day. How was

yours?" I asked with a smile. It felt good not to ask via text. I'd been dying to ask him ever since I'd finished work, but I didn't want to arrive at our date having already used up the portfolio of questions I had at hand ready to ask him.

"Not as good as yours, but it was alright––glad I was able to do an early shift for once. I know it's cheesy, but sitting here with you now, my day has got a whole lot better," he said with sincerity, sending shivers down my spine and allowing goosebumps to take up residence on my bare arms.

Normally, we were ships passing in the night, only speaking for a few hours in between our work. Just after I'd finish at the office, he'd be heading to the club to work a night shift.

"You're so smooth." I took a small sip of my whiskey and coke, and relaxed back into my seat. "Are there any promotions on the horizon for you?"

"Hopefully assistant manager soon, but one day I'd love to run the place. What about you? Reckon you'll be a partner at the firm any time soon?"

I paused and thought about his question for a second. Would I be happy to become a partner, or even a senior associate? Absolutely. I loved helping my clients and fighting for justice, and I was paid well to do it. But, my dreams didn't end with my career. I imagined being able to travel the world. I'd already saved up almost enough money to take a break from work, and in a few more years I'd have more than enough to take someone with me. Maybe I could take Connor, if we worked out.

"I'd love to be a partner for the firm I work at, if they'll let me return when I leave in a few years."

"Why are you gonna leave?"

"Ever since I was a little girl, I've wanted to see the world. I want to go back to my grandparents' farm in The Netherlands. I want to explore concrete jungles and run across beaches covered in white sand. I want to see the stars in the southern hemisphere where they make the sky as bright as it could ever get. It's also a bit embarrassing that I have a travel journal, something I started to make when I was a small child."

Travelling made me smile more than anything in the world. I could remember running through my grandparents' tulip fields as a child, rolling around amongst the flowers, their pollen filling the air as I disturbed their peace. It had been over twenty years since they'd passed. That memory was all I had of them, especially as my parents had moved to the UK after selling their farm. I was determined to go back, if only to feel as alive as I had as a child. Free and not tied down––no responsibility––just love for everyone and everything around me.

"That's not embarrassing at all. Your plans sound incredible. I know I've only known you for around two months, but from what I've seen so far, you aren't the type of person to sit back and allow that dream not to become a reality."

"You're smoother than I thought." I smirked at him, ready for him to laugh sarcastically back, but instead he threw up his arms as if he was surrendering to me there and then.

"Hey, I'm just being honest."

Our evening seemed to draw to a close quicker than I'd expected as time ran away from us. We smiled, didn't stop talking and laughed through tears, all while consuming enough food and drink to last a whole day in just a few hours. It was perfect.

We stood outside the bar and somehow there seemed to be more people there than before. The world carried on around us, as we held on to each other, ready to say our goodbyes. In our embrace, I knew I wasn't ready to go home, to say farewell to the warmth of him on that mild spring night, because nobody ever wants to wake up from a good dream. It was like I was living in a fairy tale and I was about to get my happily ever after. However, I didn't want the film to draw to a close. I wanted to live in my moment forever. Why? Because why stop at the good part? I hoped that evening was the start of my true happiness, and I couldn't wait to continue living it.

His arms pulled me away from his chest, so my eyes looked up to meet his. I couldn't edge away from his gaze, those of a gentle giant stood above me, even though I wanted to––to look at his lips, his stubbled jaw-line and eyelashes anyone would desire. I just hoped he felt the same as he looked at me.

"I'm going to kiss you now."

I hummed in response.

I closed my eyes as his lips met mine.

In that moment, as my eyes fell shut, I was all his. I was as happy as that little girl rolling around in a field full of flowers.

Chapter One

"I'm off now. Make sure you aren't here too much longer," Janine said as she tapped away at her phone without looking up for very long.

"I'm right behind you." I smiled as she made her way to the elevator.

It was weird having an assistant. It had only been five years since I'd been promoted to an associate at the firm––five years of hard work, late nights and arse-kissing, but it had all been worth it. Then, a year ago, I'd become a senior associate at Howarth and Co, with my very own assistant and a prestigious corner office. I hadn't envisaged progressing so much in my career in such a short space of time, not with my sights set on travelling, but I'd never been the type of person to pass up an opportunity.

Was it a good move? I was thinking not. As each day went by, I'd learnt more about the firm than I ever wanted to. I was helping my clients, being their voice and standing up for them in court, and although that hadn't changed, the type of clients I could represent had. It turned out all that mattered was money. Our new clients had to fit our brand—exclusivity and money. Lots of money. I was starting to believe I wasn't even a fit for the brand.

If all of that wasn't enough, I barely saw Connor. We continued to be passing ships, even after being together five years and living together.

When are you coming home? I miss you x

I glanced at my phone in between my last meeting and the time I'd set aside to work through some papers. I barely had time to breathe, never mind to type out a response to tell him when I'd be home—why I was never at home—why I was hardly ever in the arms of my man. I should have replied, because I did miss him. He'd become more important than my career, even if sometimes it didn't seem that way.

I poured myself a coffee from the overused machine in my office, one that was meant for clients that I could never resist. I looked out across the cityscape, the tall buildings glowing as they hid the oranges of the sunset behind them. The hum of the coffee machine became a distant noise as I sat at my desk, with paperwork scattered all over it, and imagined being in a far away land––somewhere I could be carefree but allow my senses to run wild––different smells, flowers as colourful as a rainbow and a whole world of different sights I could set my eyes on. I'd saved up enough money to travel two years prior, but I'd put it off because the time hadn't been right. It hadn't been right for Connor as he'd become one of the managers of the club a year and a half ago, nor was it right for my career when I'd received my promotion. I couldn't help but wonder how different my life might have been if I'd given up and left all those years ago. What I did know was that I was all but ready to hand in my notice and leave. It was pre-written and locked away in my desk for the right moment.

I couldn't wait to see the world, my hands

wrapped in Connor's, exploring the places I'd dreamed of since I was a little girl.

A vibration on the desk pulled me from a long daydream. My eyes still glazed over, I picked up my phone without looking at the screen.

"Hello," I muttered, still staring into a blank space in my mind.

"So, you're alive then?" Sarcasm rolled off Connor's tongue effortlessly. "Why haven't you been answering my texts?"

"Babe, I've been with clients and catching up on paperwork."

"Oh, I know, and whenever you're at work, I don't exist. It's nearly eight. It's dark. We've not had dinner together in over two weeks now." He spoke with anger at first, his voice raised, until he paused for a second and his words became softer. "I miss you. I miss sitting and having food with you in the evening. I feel lost without hearing about your day, watching you down a glass of wine, before I head out to work myself."

I looked behind me where the orange hues of the sky had now faded into darkness.

"You know I've got to concentrate when I'm at work. I need to focus and show my clients compassion, show them that someone does care and wants to listen to them in their darkest of hours. I don't ever forget about you. How could I? You're my number one."

"Can we please try harder, then? It seems the longer we spend in our relationship, the less I see you. I don't think I could go on never seeing the person I love." I knew by the way he said *we*, he meant *me*. He wanted me to try harder, because it was my fault. It was my job's fault. He did have a point. We barely saw each other anymore, and although I loved him with all my heart, I'd been ignoring the cracks appearing in our relationship. It was all the more reason for us to escape to another part of the world and just be free from responsibility, to find ourselves. Honestly, I couldn't wait to be free to love him even more than I already did.

"I'll be home soon. I'm just packing up my things now. Do you want me to grab any food on the way home?" I asked, without saying sorry. Apologising would be admitting that my work ethic was wrong, which it wasn't. My parents had raised me with cast iron focus and determination to achieve anything I set my mind on. I couldn't apologise for that, because I could work and still love him; there was room for both.

"No, I'm good, sweetie. I love you," his rough voice hummed down the phone.

"I love you, too."

I placed the phone down once I could only hear silence and then rested my head on the cold glass table—partly out of exhaustion, partly out of frustration that he just didn't understand.

Not long until we can run away together.

I lifted my head and allowed my eyes to adjust to the bright office lights, which illuminated the window behind me for the whole of London to see. I packed my things into my handbag before ordering an Uber. The building was eerily quiet as usual at that time of night, with only a few people still glued to their computers. I pressed the ground floor button in the elevator and stood alone, turning to my reflection in the mirror. My hair, once tied up in a precise bun, had started to become loose, with light and dark browns falling to the grey of my suit jacket. My eyes were starting to show how worn they really were. Despite claiming to provide twenty-four hour coverage, my foundation definitely didn't on a woman my age. The doors opened out to the main lobby, an airy space as clean and white as a new hospital without the smell.

"I wondered when I'd be seeing you. I thought you may have snuck out without me saying goodnight." I turned to Ward, the office security guard, who always met me with a smile. He was the perfect medicine after my phone call with Connor.

"I'd never sneak out. Your smiles are too endearing for me to try to avoid."

"You're too kind, Miss Jansen."

"Not kind, just honest, and for the billionth time, call me Fleur." Ward had a habit of being too formal in the few years he'd worked there. He wasn't a friend as such, but he always brightened my day.

"Yes, Miss... I mean, Fleur." A cheeky grin grew on his face, and with a swift nod, I stepped out of the lobby and onto the pedestrianised street. A cold rush of wind brushed my cheeks as I tracked my Uber's arrival on my phone. Once I left the shelter of the building, rain battered my face, each droplet feeling like an icicle piercing my skin.

I kept my head down, tracing the same footsteps I took daily to where my Uber would pick me up. A few drunks staggered in front of me, something I'd seen more and more of the later I stayed at the office.

I heard a whistle behind me, the type women had heard from builders on building sites in the nineteen-fifties, so my heels clicked faster as I picked up my pace.

"I'd love to have a good go on your tits." His words were slurred as he stumbled in my vicinity. I didn't know whether to laugh or cry as the creep moved closer forcing me to move faster and faster. Not even Connor had been near my boobs recently, so a guy smelling of cheap booze with a whole lot of unwarranted confidence due to his beer-goggles had no chance. If there had been more people around us I would have confronted the sexism that oozed so effortlessly from his mouth, but as the sky was only lit dimly by the moon and I was alone, I naturally ran.

It was like a rerun of Bambi learning to walk, wobbling as I tried to find some balance. I didn't have to run far, with my Uber waiting in the distance, but I stopped in my tracks a good few metres away when I heard the distinct sound of a woman crying.

I looked to my side to see someone sitting on the floor, surrounded by two men. One of them had a bottle of beer in his hand while the other attempted to pick the woman up from the ground. I could see him straining with force as the woman pulled in the opposite direction. I ran over, but not before looking behind me to find the guy still stumbling to find his feet, muttering in the distance.

"Get away from her!" I yelled as I approached the side street where the woman had curled herself into a ball like a primary school child in P.E. Both men glanced at me before running into the distance, away from the glow of the street lamp and into the darkness.

I was met by a middle-aged woman who sat sobbing silently, like she had so much emotion but nothing left to give. She looked as though she'd been dragged from Hyde Park to Canary Wharf, through the streets of London by her hair. Her skin looked grey and dull under the dim lighting of the streets, and her clothes were worn with stains. Her eyes were the saddest I'd ever seen, and I'd seen plenty of them as a solicitor.

"Are you okay?" I crouched down to her level and watched her cringe in pain as she moved to look at me. I could tell she'd been crying as her eyes raged a dark red, even though the rain tried in vain to conceal her tears. "What are you doing here?"

"My children." Her voice croaked as it battled the lump in her throat.

"What about your children?" My hand met hers as it shivered in the cold and she moved stiffly, as though she were in agony.

"My husband. He's taken the kids. I don't know where they are. My children." She started to sob as though images of her children filled her mind.

I looked back to see the drunk approaching us, given extra time by the zig-zags he made across the path. I gestured to get the woman up, but she didn't move. I had to pull her with force, using both of my arms. Her body hung limply, showing none of the resistance she'd given the men.

"Come on, let's get you to my cab. You can't stay here."

I led her to my Uber. She held onto me with her arm resting over my shoulders, and her hand held on for dear life. Whatever was going on with her, I wasn't about to let her sit, drenched and vulnerable, on the street. I wasn't about to let her give up.

"What's your name?" I asked as I acted as a walking aid for her feeble body.

"Andrea."

"Come on, Andrea. Let's get you somewhere safe." I opened the Uber door and tried not to let her collapse against the seats.

"Can you lock your doors and circle the block? My destination may have changed. I'll pay extra," I asked, and with a swift nod from the driver we pulled away from the drunks of London. As each second passed, I had more and more questions about what had led Andrea to the streets, but that didn't matter right now. All that mattered was that she was safe.

Chapter Two

"Andrea?" I waved in front of her face to bring her out of a daze, similar to the one I'd ended up in at the office. She remained silent, still and emotionless aside from the tears rolling down her face.

Andrea's clothes hung off her with the weight of the rain, dripping across the leather seats in the back on the Uber.

A cherry scent lingered in the cab from an air-freshener, which helped to mask her damp smell. The car lit up then faded into darkness every few seconds, each time we drove under another street light, like frames in an old motion picture. The difference, though, was that Andrea wasn't moving. She was frozen. Numb.

"Andrea? Why were you sitting outside in this freezing weather?" It was cold enough that even I should have been wearing more layers.

She croaked inaudibly, the sound lost in the roaring of the engine.

"What was that?" I moved in closer, to where the cherry air-freshener had little to no impact. Andrea turned her head slowly, her face looking as it had the first time I'd seen her. Defeat. She had given up.

"What else am I supposed to do? I can't get into my house. My husband took my children." Her chest started to huff as she struggled to catch her breath, going from a moment of serenity in her daze into a flurry of panic.

"Okay. Take deep breaths. I'm going to help you. I'm a solicitor. Start from the beginning. No rush." I remained calm––her equilibrium, her stability, as if she were a ship in the middle of a storm as it rocked her almost to the point of tipping over.

"My husband and I have been going through a rough patch, but we were trying to work through it."

She cleared her throat and looked at me, almost like she was seeing if she'd divulged enough information, and then continued when she realised she hadn't. "I found out he was cheating on me, but for the sake of our children, we had to work it out. I mean, that's all my life revolves around: him and them."

I listened to her every word, each one painting a picture in my mind. She barely made eye contact, like talking to anyone but her husband and children was hard for her.

"He told me to go to the shop, said we needed a few things and gave me some cash. So I did. I came home about half an hour later and they were gone. My children. I had nothing but the shopping. I didn't have my keys and the house was locked up. I didn't even have my phone. I tried to break one of the windows to get into the house, but after cutting myself I knew I was just wasting time." Goosebumps rose on my arms at the thought of her life being torn apart in the space of half an hour. I winced a little as she pulled her long-sleeved t-shirt up to show me a large cut on her wrist.

"Have you spoken with the police?"

"I couldn't. I have no phone. I don't even know what I'd say to them. I can barely think straight. I just found myself walking, and then it started raining. The more it rained, the more I wanted to give up." No wonder she looked tired. What had been hours must have felt like days. "I don't know what I can do, other than give up."

"Andrea, I can assure you right now, you have plenty of options––we do." I smiled and squeezed her hand a little tighter to reassure her that everything was going to be okay. I couldn't take away her pain, the memories of that day, but I could try to make it right.

"Thank you." Her eyes filled with tears once more. "What's the plan? What do I need to do?" She lifted her shoulders that had been slumped the whole time.

"Legally speaking, your husband is fine to take your children because he has parental responsibility. However, he should have gained consent from you first. That won't look too great for him in court. I believe the best course of action is to apply for a Seek and Find Order so we can determine where he and the children are, and then serve him with Residence Order papers. I think you've got a good case here and I'm going to represent you. I'll fight tooth and nail if that's what it takes to get you back with your children. Then you would need to determine the fate of your relationship with Mr..." I couldn't assume she'd want nothing more to do with her husband. Divorce was often as big a decision as marriage, and from what she had told me, she'd been trying to save it. Personally, I knew if I were in her position, I wouldn't have been able to forgive such a thing.

"Palmer, his name is Steven Palmer." She spoke with confidence, the strongest I'd seen her. "Cheating on me is one thing, but to take away my children, my house, leaving me with nothing—barely a shred of my dignity as I had a breakdown and smashed the windows of my own home—I want to kick that bastard where it hurts. I want the house. My children's home."

In my line of work, I'd seen all manner of people, but never someone so full of emotion. Maybe it was because I'd seen Andrea in her most vulnerable state. I looked at her—a fierce woman with her spark finally starting to ignite, a force to be reckoned with—and I almost started to feel sorry for what was about to come to her husband.

"You don't need to worry. We'll get your children back, but before we do anything, we need to get you sorted for the night. We can deal with getting you into your home tomorrow, but you need to get some rest. Come and see me in my office tomorrow at 2pm." I handed her my business card, which had my address on it. "In the meantime, Whitechapel has a phone I'm sure you'll be able to reach me on if you have any worries or concerns." I nodded to Andrea and simultaneously to the driver. "Let's get you to Whitechapel."

The light that had appeared in Andrea's eyes quickly diminished at the thought of being helped by a charity—by a homeless shelter. That spark I'd started to see come back had faded into black. She was a hollow shell sitting helplessly on a beach—empty and shivering with cold, each wave leaving her battered and bruised and each ebb taking another piece of her away.

I took my phone out of my bag and was about to dial ahead to Whitechapel. Another message filled with question marks from Connor blinked on the screen. Andrea's head dropped and she shook her head in disagreement.

"I can't go to... a homeless shelter."

"Why not?" I placed my phone back in my bag, ignoring the persistent calls that continued to come through, making my bag vibrate in sync with my phone.

"I have a house for Christ's sake—I just can't get in it." Her voice raised slightly, like she was angry. Angry at the only person wanting to help her. "I don't want charity. There are other people who need that place more than I do."

"And you're probably right, but you need to get cleaned up. You need a good rest if we're ever going to get your kids back and safe with you. You need to do this for them." Andrea looked at me, hearing words she didn't want to hear as she'd already made up her mind. She wasn't going to Whitechapel and I couldn't force her, but my work here wasn't done.

"Driver, can you take us to our destination now? Can you take us home?"

The driver nodded as I wrapped my hand around Andrea's. It was freezing to touch. I looked at her and gave her a small smile.

I knew that taking her home was ethically wrong, something a solicitor shouldn't do. That was one thing I'd always had a problem with—keeping work separate —because it was my entire life. Was I worried about the partners of the firm finding out? No, not really. Any decent human being would have done the same as me, because if I wasn't representing her, it would be ethically right. All that stood in the way of a warm shower and some good company was a bit of red tape, and I wasn't afraid of tearing it down. What I was afraid of? Connor's reaction.

"Everything is going to be okay."

Chapter Three

After a short drive, the Uber pulled into my road alongside the row of Georgian houses that lined it. The grey brick and large white windows of the buildings made the area one of the most sought after in London. I'd lived there ever since I'd graduated from university, but wouldn't have been able to if it hadn't been for my parents who rented the property out to me at what they called *mates rates*. Each month, I sent their low rent payment, and each month I became that little bit closer to being able to travel the world.

My parents and I had a weird relationship. We had a strong bond formed by our blood that tied us together, but I saw them about as often as a solar eclipse, mostly because they spent more time on cruises than they did on dry land.

I could see a Connor shaped shadow in the window and the blinds were pinched apart as he peered out into the street at the sound of the car pulling up. He was expecting me, and had been for a few hours, but I was sure he wasn't expecting to see Andrea.

I stepped out of the Uber as gracefully as I could in a pencil skirt that matched my grey jacket, and ushered Andrea out of the vehicle. I looked up to the window nervously and smiled––a pathetic attempt to put out the fire before it had even been lit, but it was too dark for him to see my facial expressions. The minute Andrea appeared from the vehicle, the blinds snapped back together.

Oh boy.

My heels thumped against the varnished wood floor, with Andrea's footsteps sounding almost like a tip-toe compared to mine.

"I'll take your coat, and if you go through that door and into the kitchen, I'll make you some food."

"You're too kind. Thank you." Andrea practically curtsied and scurried through the kitchen as I opened the door into the living area to face Connor.

I didn't get a chance to defend myself or my actions, because the minute the door was ajar, Connor opened his mouth.

"What have I told you, Fleur? You can't keep bringing home clients when you feel sorry for them!"

"I tried to get her to go to the shelter, I really did, but she sat helplessly in the—"

Before I could finish, he interrupted. One of his hands was braced angrily on the wall and I watched his veins bulge as he yelled some more. The other hand ran through the brown strands of his hair in frustration.

"Why do I not believe you? You said you'd stop bringing clients home after I moved in. This is the third time."

"I'm sorry. I just couldn't leave her. I can't let someone sit in the rain in this cold and be molested by every drunk or creep that walks past." Each word was like armour that protected me from what was about to come. It was a defence mechanism I often wore at work but something I rarely had to use with Connor.

"We might as well rent out the spare room to these people. At least then we'd make some fucking money. And then, maybe, just maybe, I wouldn't have to put up with drunk people for a living and you could work for the both of us in the job you never seem to want to come home from."

Five years ago, he'd enjoyed his job––loved it, even. Then, as each day had passed, he'd despised it a little more, but he'd continued to work through it. I'd told him so many times to find a new job because each night he went to work and came home a little less of the person I'd first met in that bar.

"You know, the job you seem to live in every minute and every second of every single God-damned day because that's all you know how to do." *Ouch.* His words cut deep through my armour as he ignored me and everything I had to say on the matter. He was mad.

"Can you keep your voice down? I do have a life," I said, another pathetic attempt at defending myself.

"You don't. When was the last time you saw a friend outside of work? Or the last time we sat down with your parents for a meal?" *A long time.* I had Janine, but we never went out for a drink or met up for shopping because I was her boss. "You live to work, and your life shouldn't be like that. When are you actually going to be the Fleur you aspired to be all those years ago, when we first got talking? You always said your job was going to serve your ultimate purpose, yet it seems like you're the one serving work." So many more questions, so much interrogation, I didn't know where to start, aside from apologising like I did every time.

"I'm sorry," I said under my breath, but it went ignored.

"I feel forgotten about. All those months of you wanting day trips and evening meals, for me to meet your parents and go on holidays. Then, you went quiet. You don't care about anything other than work."

"Look, I'm sorry. I promise my priorities will change, but for tonight, it's not going to. We have a guest, someone who has real problems, so keep your damn voice down or get out." I'd boiled over. I was a simmering pot, and each insult he spewed added more heat, which allowed my anger to spill over the sides.

Connor's expression changed. His eyebrows, once pointed in anger, straightened as sadness took over. He swept past me, pushing the door open, and grabbed his coat from the hallway coat rack before storming out. The heavy wooden door slammed behind him, making the whole house shake.

I stood, mouth agape, stunned that Connor had left. It wasn't like him, or us for that matter. We had our lovers' tiffs like any other couple. We argued about having different views in life, but not once had he stormed out. I shook my head and redirected my energy into something that mattered more than a stupid argument: Andrea.

"I'm so sorry." Andrea leapt up from a kitchen stool as I walked into the room, immediately apologising for the drama she thought she'd caused. But her causing this drama was far from the truth, because I was the drama, and Connor couldn't escape that.

"Don't be silly. He'll probably be back before you go to bed. I'm sure he's just cooling off in a bar or something." I may have been able to drink my colleagues under the table, but with Connor, I'd met my match. I blamed it on the fact he'd worked in pubs and bars all his life. The amount of drinks he'd been bought by women wearing swimming costumes, something they apparently considered suitable outfits for a night out, had built up his tolerance. "Look, it's too late to cook now. How about you go get showered and changed, and I'll order us some food? Is Chinese alright?" I asked and started walking back out of the kitchen towards the stairs, offering a swift nod to Andrea so she knew to follow.

"Are you sure? I will pay you back as soon as I'm back on my feet." Andrea followed, her head still hanging in despair.

"Pshhh. I don't want to hear any of that. You're my guest."

Once we were up the stairs, I pulled open a heavy, wooden wardrobe, pulling out a nightdress that would fit her. Luckily, her build was similar to mine—small and curvy. That's what I'd been told by Connor.

"Now, the shower is through there. Help yourself to shower gel and shampoo. When you're done, get changed and bring down your clothes for the wash. I'll put them on a wash and dry cycle so they're ready for tomorrow." I gave Andrea one last smile before starting to turn around, stopping in my tracks when her delicate hand held onto my arm.

"Thank you. You honestly have no idea how much this means." She pulled me in towards her chest, holding onto me as tightly as anyone ever had—holding on for dear life.

Before long, I'd ordered the food, set the gleaming white plates on the table and texted Connor asking where he was. Of course, he didn't reply. I didn't really expect him to, but I took the steps necessary to show him that I cared.

Andrea quietly tiptoed down the stairs and slipped through to the dining room just off the kitchen like a ninja, making me jump as she appeared out of nowhere. Her skin looked rejuvenated and was a blushing pink. The colour in her face had started to return and she shed a small smile, like the shower had washed away her pain. There was a beautiful woman hiding behind all the hurt and dirt. I could see that now.

"How do you feel?"

"I definitely needed that, thank you." Andrea perched on a kitchen stool and watched me pour myself the glass of wine I was in desperate need of.

"Want one?" I asked, and with a small nod from her, I grabbed another long-stemmed glass with a large bowl and allowed the red liquid to flow.

I watched her take a sip after swirling the glass around a little. It clearly wasn't her first time drinking wine as she acted like some sort of wine connoisseur, oozing confidence and being the real Andrea.

"Look at you, swirling the glass like a professional."

"Ha, yeah. Steven liked his wine. Anyway, we've spent most of the evening focused on me and..." She gulped, not wanting to bring the words to the tip of her tongue. "Tell me about you? What's your life like? Let me live someone else's life for a second."

She wrapped her hands around the bowl of the glass and leant in a little to me. Her eyes glistened under the kitchen spotlights.

"Okay, I've been a solicitor for many years now."

"Not work. You, personally. Tell me about you. What do you love? Where are you from? What are your wildest dreams?" Andrea interrupted again.

I blushed.

"Oh, well, I love wine." I laughed, lifting the glass and clinking it against hers. "I lived in The Netherlands as a child then moved to London for my father's work. One day, I want to go back there. I have a bit of a travel bug if I'm honest, except I don't want to go away and relax. I want to travel––meet incredible people, experience different cultures and forget about life back home for a while." My head dropped a little and my voice softened. "One day," I muttered. "But, enough about me."

"Why do I get the feeling you don't get asked about yourself very often?" she asked, looking directly at me.

Because people knew all there was to know about me. The evening continued, as we ate and allowed the Cabernet Sauvignon to dye our lips a deep red. I missed having fun, having a friend to talk to. The smiles and laughter from both of us filled me with so much warmth, but it turned ice cold at the sound of the front door slamming. He had come back for me, like I'd known he would. I just hoped we could move on from this, because I loved him, undeniably.

Chapter Four

That evening, I lay in bed next to Connor, feeling the furthest away from him I'd ever felt. I'd endured the silence when he'd arrived back home smelling of lager. I'd even put up with the disappointed looks as he'd stood under the door frame while I'd made up the guest bedroom for Andrea. He'd smiled at her whenever she'd looked over, and that shred of empathy he had shown her? That was the man I'd fallen in love with. It wasn't her fault she'd come here; it was mine, and I was certainly paying for it.

On the odd occasion we did find ourselves in bed at the same time, we didn't want to let each other go. Our skin would touch, clammy and uncomfortable, our lips only parting to find our breaths. But that night, there was nothing, no matter how much I tried to push my rear against his hip, grazing it against the boxer shorts he'd unusually kept on. Not even a deep sigh, a moan or groan got a reaction. At that point, I had more chance of having sex with Andrea, never mind a conversation.

All I wanted was reassurance that he was okay—that we were both okay.

"I'm sorry," Connor muttered under his breath. *Finally, he speaks.* His voice was low, yet the sound still echoed within our bedroom, underneath the high ceiling.

"You don't need to be sorry. I understand why you needed a breather," I said, turning to face him. His eyes looked sad, dimly lit by the moonlight creeping its way through the blinds, but he wasn't looking at me. He was staring into space.

"No. I know that. I'm just really struggling..." He spoke softly.

"Whatever it is, I'm here. We can work through it together. Is it the bar?"

"You aren't listening to me. I wasn't finished." He was still looking blankly above, as if he could see through the ceiling, the roof and out into the night sky. I sat up in bed and secured the duvet in my arm pits, turning to get a better look at him. "I guess that's the problem, because I don't feel like you've been listening to me for a while now. It's been sounding over and over in my head constantly, and it kills me to think that I'm not sure I can go on any longer, continuing the way we currently are."

"Wha... What are you trying to say?" Bile rose to my throat as I choked on my words.

"I'm saying I love you, but I need more, because at the moment I feel like I'm holding onto the woman I fell in love with five years ago instead of the woman you are now. I want to hold onto you—all of you. Even the work obsessed Fleur—the drives me up the wall Fleur—but maybe just a little less of the work all day and night, and brings clients home Fleur. Okay?"

Tears built up and puddled on my eyelids, knowing full well that I'd hurt him. My priorities had been in the wrong place all along—working for a firm that only cared about money and not me or their clients, shrugging off my dreams of travelling and not putting myself first.

That was all about to change.

I nodded and sniffed, and made myself small, curling up as close as was physically possible to him. His arm shuffled underneath and pulled me in tighter. I'd almost forgotten I could be that close to someone. His warm lips pressed lightly on my neck as he pushed my hair to one side, and I trembled underneath his touch.

"Try to get some sleep. I'm sure you've got a big day ahead tomorrow with all your clients," he whispered softly into my ear.

I smiled, although he couldn't see, and shut my eyes, not moving an inch—just lying in his embrace.

The next morning, my routine was the same as usual. I got dressed while Connor snoozed in bed, and grabbed a mixed-berry smoothie from the fridge for breakfast. The only difference was making sure Andrea was able to keep herself busy until her appointment with me at two o'clock that afternoon.

With all of that taken care of, I stepped into the office lobby, fighting my way through crowds to get the elevator up to my floor.

"Good morning, Fleur," Janine said with a bounce in her step, handing me a brown file filled with the day's briefs. "There is a fresh, hot coffee on your desk waiting for you."

"You are literally the best assistant anyone could ever ask for. Has anyone ever told you that?" I said, flicking through the file as my stride continued on auto-pilot to my office.

"It's been mentioned a few times." She giggled to herself and then started to brief me on today's clients. "Your nine-thirty meeting has been rescheduled to tomorrow to make way for a new client, orders from the boss. There aren't any details aside from a name. Mr Steven Palmer. "

Palmer. It couldn't be.

"Where is the boss?" I asked Janine, and she swiftly pointed across to one of the boardrooms.

My legs carried me as quickly as they could towards the boardroom, all while I prepared myself mentally to deal with Walter. He'd fire me on the spot if I ever used his first name in work. I guessed that was why Ward was always apprehensive about calling me Fleur.

I pressed open the door slightly and pushed my head through.

"Mr Howarth, can I have a quick word?"

"Ah, Fleur, of course. I have a few minutes before my meeting," he said pleasantly.

"This appointment you've put in my diary, with a Mr Steven Palmer?"

"Yes, he's a very good friend of mine from college. He currently works for Cybrex, you know…"

"Yes, I know the one. The big tech firm we've been trying to get on our books for the past year." I'd had a feeling Cybrex would come up in conversation some way or another, but I hadn't expected to be asked to represent Steven, the man allegedly responsible for adultery and taking Andrea's children.

"Well, this case could seal that deal, and I know both Steven and Cybrex will be in great hands with you representing them." He coughed into a tissue and wiped his mouth, then smiled and continued to look through his files while our tech guy continued to set up the projector no one ever seemed to get the hang of.

I couldn't look Walter directly in his eyes, and I nervously wiped my palm on my dress. I dreaded what was about to come out of my mouth and feared what would come out of his in response.

"I can't," I said abruptly.

"I'm sorry?" He looked up but my eyes still avoided his. He was likely glaring at me.

"Sorry, sir, but I'm afraid that's not possible. You see…" I paused and caught a glimpse of his death stare. I was fired. "I've already agreed to represent his wife."

I'm fired. I'm fired. I'm well and truly fired.

"You mean to tell me that you are representing the woman Steven found in bed with another man?" Walter nudged the desk with his stomach as he stood up and towered over it. "When did you agree to represent her?"

"Is that what he told you? I found Andrea in absolute bits. She told me how he had been cheating on her, and how she was trying to fix the relationship for the sake of the children, but he decided to take the children away from the marital home, leaving her with nothing."

Walter looked at me in disbelief and I didn't know what to do with myself. I looked around the room nervously, not knowing what else to say as he continued to look, but now with disappointment.

"Fleur, you're a great solicitor, one of my best, but your one downfall is that you're too trusting. You've allowed someone to cloud your judgement, and good solicitors should be able to represent their clients without wearing their hearts on their sleeves."

"Is that not what you're doing with Steven? You've not heard Andrea's side of the story. In fact, you seem completely satisfied that he's telling the truth." My tongue spiked in an attack, and I instantly regretted the tone I used.

"I think you need to take a deep breath, go to your office and meet Steven," Walter said professionally, trying not to lose his temper. "It will be good for you to hear his side of the story, and then you can put that insanely large brain of yours to use, weighing up the pros and cons of each client, along with both of their very convincing stories, and decide which client would serve the best interests of the company. When you've done that, I'll help you put a case together for Steven."

Smug bastard. I wanted to argue with him. I wanted to tell him I wasn't going to meet with Steven, but he was right and I needed to prove to him that I was a good solicitor—a solicitor who could make unclouded, impartial decisions.

"Yes, Sir." That's all I could say to him before I marched out of the conference room to my office, bumping into my assistant on the way.

"Is everything okay?" Janine asked as I stormed behind my desk and sat down with force, as if my actions and the fact that I was red in the face didn't answer her question.

"Not really. I'm fed up with working in this dog-eat-dog world. I'm fed up with having to answer to someone who only cares about money. I'm even more fed up that in order to be successful, I need to change

—I need to be a robotic arsehole with no emotion or compassion for people who come into my life."

Janine looked at me aimlessly and then rushed to the coffee machine, doing the only thing she knew would help in that situation, despite her only pouring me a coffee just minutes before.

I took a sip and sat, watching the clock, waiting for the devil himself to walk through the door—waiting for Steven to try and prove me wrong.

Chapter Five

"Mr Palmer has arrived. Shall I send him in?" Janine's voice echoed through the phone. It would have been quicker for her to come in and tell me, as my office was directly opposite her desk, along with the lifts and the reception.

"Yes please, thanks, Janine," I said and braced myself, clearing my throat ready to introduce myself to him.

Moments later, in walks Andrea's husband. He

was physically attractive, a little older than I had placed Andrea. His short hair was brushed with silvers and greys, his skin clear of any imperfection, and his frame held onto his suit perfectly. I even found myself trying to find his abs underneath his white shirt, and when I couldn't find them, I was picturing them instead.

"You must be Fleur. I'm Mr Palmer, but you can call me Steve." He held his hand out to me politely. He had an irresistible swagger about him that the average woman would have found hard to resist.

Oh, I know who you are.

"Steve, an absolute pleasure." My hand met his. His skin was soft and delicate, a giveaway that he'd never done a hard day of physical graft, if I hadn't already known he was in the tech industry. "Walter has given me a little overview, but please do tell me how I can help."

"Well, where do I start?" he asked rhetorically, and then ran his tongue slowly across his lips, forcing my attention to them. "I've been married to Andrea, my wife, for just over seven years and we have two young children, but I'm sure you know that already."

I tensed up at his accusation. "Why do you say that? What makes you think I know all this?" I said rigidly, immediately regretting each and every word.

"I just assumed Walter would have told you?" He

raised an eyebrow and paused for a second before continuing. "The reason I'm here is because my wife has been cheating on me. I took the children to my parents' house and I want to file for divorce."

"That's all well and good, but why did you take the children from the family home?" I asked, making notes on my laptop in front of me.

"I caught my wife cheating on me with another man in my own home, while the children were there, and I was working. Well, I was working, but I came home early to surprise her and the kids. She invited a stranger into our home. I don't know how long her cheating has been going on and I don't want to know, but when I told her I wanted a divorce, when I told her I wanted her to leave, she got aggressive. She hit me, she threw stuff at me, she even broke our glass coffee table. I took the kids to my parents' house to keep them safe."

He seemed genuine, but I couldn't help but think back to the pain Andrea was in, how hurt she was, and everything she'd told me. I wanted to ask him so many questions, but I couldn't without him knowing I'd met Andrea. The company would lose Steve as a client, and Walter would lose a friend. Heck, I would probably even lose my job, which sounded more and more appealing the more Steve spoke. I continued to look up at him every now and then before quickly returning to type on my laptop.

"Look, she's not a bad mum. I'd even go as far as saying I still love her. What isn't there to love aside from the adultery? She loves our children, she'd do anything for them, and she's a stunner—absolutely gorgeous. The best looking mum on the playground. The perkiest boobs you'd—"

"I'm going to stop you there," I interrupted, as he looked down at my chest and then back up with a grin the size of the Cheshire Cat.

"All I'm trying to say is that she can see the kids, but I want a divorce and I want what's mine. The house. The kids' house."

"Why do you say the house is yours?"

"We wouldn't be in it if it wasn't for my income. She doesn't work."

I looked at the self-entitled man and stood up, pulling down my dress to avoid giving him a glimpse of something he may have liked.

"First off, Mr Palmer, when we look at marital assets and splitting them, we consider income but we also consider marital contribution in the form of child care. Your wife may not have been out of work by choice. She could argue that she's been the home-maker since the time you were married, and that would carry some weight. Secondly, to do my job well, I need to trust my client. What if Andrea gets legal representation, and she states, I don't know, that you've been cheating? How can I trust you're telling me the truth when you've been flirting with me since you walked through that door?" I stood up and looked directly at him, like I would a judge in court, awaiting his response.

Steven stood up, pulling at the sleeves of his suit, straightening up his appearance. He slowly walked around the table, and stood inches from me.

"Because, Fleur, if I can be in a room with a gorgeous lady like yourself for ten minutes without jumping on you, I'm sure I can navigate life without jumping on every other woman I see."

I was angry. Furious.

"Steven, great to see you. How's things?" Steven winked and stepped backwards before turning to greet Walter.

Saved by Walter.

His head had been about to be smashed through the office window. Who was I kidding? Even an inflated ego the size of his wouldn't have smashed through those windows.

"I assume you'll get everything in order for me?" He flicked a business card over to me. "Have your assistant call mine to arrange another meeting when you need me." He walked away from my office with Walter, both of them becoming a distant laugh as they stroked each other's manhoods. They were made to be friends. I was left stood with my arms crossed and full of an emotion I couldn't quite put a pin in.

I fell to my seat and sobs as deep as a river began to flow uncontrollably from me.

Never had a man made me feel so small. I'd always been able to hold my own, but not with him. Was it because I was so invested? Or because he was the exact opposite of what I'd expected? Maybe it was because I'd started to believe his story, and I didn't want to. With all my heart, I wanted him to be the liar, but I couldn't say for certain. My gut was usually right, as strong as steel and I never doubted it, yet it sat there as crude oil in my stomach.

I couldn't move or speak. I remained still, ignoring each phone call Janine took for me. I avoided any usual pleasantries, looking directly out to the busy streets of London instead of smiling at every person who walked past my office.

I was never wrong.

The more I sat there consumed by my thoughts, the more I tormented myself. All the words both Connor and Walter had said to me about not wearing my heart on my sleeve—basically caring too much for people who shouldn't matter.

You're too trusting. You live to work.

I'm holding onto the woman I fell in love with five years ago.

Had I really changed that much? Had I become this unbearable cow who only cared about work and my clients, all for a man who thought I could be a better solicitor if I didn't care too much? I couldn't even think back to my training or my first few cases to determine if I cared more now, or if I'd been a better girlfriend five years ago, because I was broken.

I turned at the sound of my phone vibrating and quickly answered at the sight of Connor's name on the screen.

"Hey, Connor." I sniffed a little and wiped my eyes in an attempt to see if wiping my tears would make me sound okay.

"Oh, you answered. I didn't expect you to. I thought you might be busy..."

"I guess it's the new me," I said, cringing a little.

"Well, that's good to hear. I was just checking in after yesterday. I've been thinking and I know I may have been a little tough, so I'm sorry. Maybe we could go out for a meal later? Being the assistant manager has its perks, and I've managed to wangle someone to cover me for the night."

I smiled down the phone, if only he could have seen.

"That sounds wonderful. I'll see you at home. Have a good day, Connor." I ended the call and opened my desk drawer to put my phone away, finding the letter of resignation I'd pre-written. My fingers ran across the envelope, apprehensive to pick it up and open it, but I did.

I skim read the letter and with each word, a fire grew in my stomach as if my gut had soldered itself back together. I knew what I had to do.

I scribbled the date in the space I'd left at the top of the letter and pushed myself up from my chair. My colleagues seemed to pass me in a blur as I walked to Walter's office. In fact, the whole scenario was a blur aside from seeing Walter's face as I handed him the envelope. I didn't hang around for too long to watch him open it, but I did throw a sarcastic smile at Steven before holding my head high and walking out of the office with all of my dignity back intact.

My power had been restored.

"Janine, can I have a word?" I asked, summoning her to my office as I quickly placed everything into the first box I found.

"What are you doing?"

"I'm leaving, with immediate effect. Under normal circumstances, I'd take you with me because you're a force of nature and I wouldn't be nearly as good a solicitor without you. However, I don't think I'll be working for a while. What I want you to do is stay in touch, especially about Andrea, but mostly because I absolutely adore you. Now, I'm sure your job is safe because they'll need an assistant for the person who replaces me, but if you do find you can't stay here, I'll give you the best reference an employer has ever seen. Also, my client, Andrea, will be coming in around two-ish. When she gets here, will you please give her this card and tell her she'll be looked after. Tell her I'm sorry." The business card was for a friend from university, a fling actually, but it hadn't worked out. He was nearly as good as me at his job, and I knew Olly would take good care of Andrea in my absence. I wasn't about to leave her in the hands of the organisation I was walking away from.

I finished packing the things in my office and stood in front of Janine, holding both of her shoulders.

"Promise you'll keep in touch, okay?"

She nodded, wiping the tears that had started to form around her eyes, before wrapping her arms around me and hugging me. I managed to stay strong, then gave her a warm smile before carrying my box to the lift and down into the lobby, trying to avoid every soul as I battled with my emotions. I even managed to avoid Ward.

I stepped out into the mildly fresh air and burst into tears.

Relief.

Regret.

All the emotion.

A huge weight had been lifted off my shoulders, but I also knew that I'd likely just ruined my legal career and had left countless clients without representation. I straightened my shoulders as it was the firm's problem now, not mine. After all, Walter wanted me to care less. Who knew? Maybe he would hire a robot to replace me.

Chapter Six

I'd hidden away from the world for two days, isolating myself from Connor and even ignoring phone calls from my parents. Me not answering my phone wasn't something that was new to them; they probably even expected it by then, assuming that work was keeping me too busy to speak to them. If only they knew.

I knew it had been two days as I'd watched the rise and fall of the sun from the comfort of my bed, and watched the moon light up each night through the bedroom window. Sleep had been a problem, with my sleep pattern resembling Connor's. Awake at night, desperate to dream and forget about the world I'd once thought I understood, then passing out with exhaustion throughout the day. My mind worked overtime, the cogs seeming to turn more than they ever had despite being out of work.

What had I done for those two days? Aside from battling with my inner-demons, I'd watched any and all programmes that had the ability to transport me away from where I was —programmes like A Place In The Sun, Cruising with Jane McDonald and even Dr Who. Although unrealistic, I couldn't help but want the T.A.R.D.I.S to turn back the hands of time and allow me to remake choices I'd made long ago. Then maybe, just maybe, life would have been a whole lot different and I wouldn't have been lying in my bed full of regret.

"The way I see it, every life is a pile of good things and... bad things. The good things don't always soften the bad things, but vice versa, the bad things don't necessarily spoil the good things or make them unimportant."

Alright, Matt Smith. Chill Out.

I flicked off the T.V. to avoid listening to his smooth, convincing voice telling me that things were okay just the way they were, but I couldn't shake the words off. They spun around in my head until I had no choice but to acknowledge them. I knew that everyone had to live through good and bad times, and that they moulded us as people. I had good things in my life, like savings and a man as dreamy as they came, who wanted me to fulfil all of my wildest dreams and fantasies. But, it was also very hard to remember all of those good things when sorrow pushed all of them into the distance. They were still there, I knew that, but not at the forefront of my mind.

I was spiralling, and all of the good I thought I knew was turning to bad. My mind taunted me.

If Connor was still holding onto the Fleur he'd met five years ago, then why would he want me now?

I tried blinking away the thoughts, closing my eyes to stop seeing, to stop reliving an exaggerated version of the pain I'd been feeling, but it wouldn't stop. My eyes were closed but my brain was alive, vivid in colour and sending signals through my nervous system, forcing my body to react—forcing me to try to convince myself it wasn't true.

I had a boyfriend who would do anything for me. *You argue more and more with him.*

He loved me and would follow me to the ends of

the earth if I asked him to. *Why would he do that? You only care about work.*

Not anymore. I didn't need to work, I had savings and a beautiful home. A home I paid a fraction of the price I should have for, thanks to my parents. I had loving parents. *Parents you never see because you don't make time for them, and they don't make time for you.*

I did, I had and I would. They'd raised me to be the person I was. The strong woman I was.

I chanted silently, battling my thoughts as they argued back until I didn't remember battling them anymore—until I drifted off to sleep in exhaustion.

———

*D*ark clouds sat in the sky, perfectly still, as I looked out of my bedroom window—the flowers weren't moving much either.

"I want to go play outside, Mummy."

"No, Petal, not today. It's going to rain soon and you'll catch a cold."

"The rain doesn't bother me. I like watching it fall onto the flowers and then trickling off, and I like looking at the bugs, watching them trying to run and hide from the rain. I'm not a bug, Mummy. I don't need to hide from the rain."

"I know, but not today. I promise you'll get to play outside before we move to London, but Mummy and Daddy are too busy now, Petal. Besides, it rains less in the UK, so you'll get to play out a lot more there."

I looked at her and smiled. I didn't want to leave the farm or my home town behind, but I knew my dad wanted to leave. He would say things like we were living in Grandma's shadows—living her life. I didn't see what was wrong with that.

There was a sharp bright light, and once it disappeared I was in bed. I could hear screaming and shouting from my parents' bedroom, my Grandma's old room.

"We can't afford to stay here. I haven't been in education and worked my whole life to not pursue my dreams of working in the financial capital of the world."

"I know but she left us this house, the farm, everything. Why would we want to leave this and all her memories behind?"

"She's gone, Maria. We need to live our own lives, not hers. It's what she would have wanted. Her memory will come with us..." My father's voice softened until I couldn't hear it anymore.

My tiny hands balled up and rubbed my eyes. They

ached and drooped as my grandma came to life right in front of me, and she sang. Her soothing voice wrapped around me like a warm hug, and all the worry and doubt of adult life drifted into the abyss. I was a child again.

"Little, little toddler, what are you doing in my garden? You are picking all my flowers, and overdoing it."

I tried to sing the rest of the song back to her, but I couldn't speak. I tried my best but no words would come out. My mouth was moving, but nothing.

I awoke suddenly, longing to hear my grandma's voice some more—wanting to sing the rest of the song to her as I had before she passed away, changing the song's original words from Mummy and Daddy to Grandma and Grandpa.

"O my dear Grandma, please don't tell Grandpa. I will go to school now, and leave your flowers." I sobbed silently, tears rolling down my face.

I sat up and my stomach growled with hunger, fasting in between the few takeaways I'd ordered over the past two days. I didn't hesitate to click the *order again* button on the app and anxiously awaited the disapproving looks of the delivery driver who probably had our address saved as a favourite by now.

I sat in bed thinking of ways to forget about abruptly leaving my job and feeling like I had no purpose. I couldn't even begin to think about ways to fix how I was feeling, not with the constant thoughts that crashed against my skull the minute I tried to think about something else. I just needed to forget—a breather—a moment to feel something else or nothing at all.

"Is this yours?" Connor opened the door slightly and held up a McDonalds bag. The room filled instantly with the smell of freshly cooked salted fries and my stomach grumbled again in anticipation. Thankfully, I'd escaped the shame of knowing whether the same delivery driver had come to our house, and that was another thing I didn't have to worry about thanks to Connor answering the door.

"It is. I know you probably didn't want any but I ordered you more chicken nuggets." I smiled as he brought the bag over to the bed, waiting to grab it off him until I'd rearranged the pillows and shuffled back into them—prime position to dig in.

"Yeah, I'm okay, thanks," Connor said, turning his nose up at the heart attack I held in my hands. "You know you really should eat something a little healthier, maybe some vegetables... No wonder you feel like you have no energy. You've not eaten properly for days."

"My Big Mac has lettuce on it." I took a huge bite and gave him a wide grin but still managed to keep the majority of the burger in my mouth.

Connor sat at the bottom of the bed and watched me shovel the food into my mouth with no shame.

"We need to do something to make you feel better. We need to get you out of these clothes you've been wearing for days, get you out of bed, and get you some fresh air."

I looked into Connor's eyes longingly, not wanting either of us to get off the bed. I wanted to say to him that if he wanted me out of these clothes, he'd have to take them off himself, but I didn't. I didn't need to. Connor realised exactly what he needed to do to make me feel something other than defeated. He crawled across the bed, approaching with caution at first, just in case he had read the room wrong. He hadn't.

"Fuck, I've missed you. You have no idea how much I want you, all of you, right now." His breath intertwined with mine and our bodies ran with sweat, eager to be free from the clothes that trapped us from pleasure. His lips and teeth ran across my neck as though he was playing my body like an instrument, and I felt every beat. Our hands fought to free each other from our clothes, and then we fell onto each other into a mind-blowing rhythm we'd deprived ourselves of for so long.

It was everything.

I wanted him more than I ever had done—for comfort, pleasure and everything else in between.

It was all I needed and more, but most of all, it allowed me to forget.

Chapter
Seven

I sat up in bed with my thoughts consumed by Connor. He was at work but my mind brought him to life right before my eyes. His fingers gently glided up from my calf to the top of my thigh, and I trembled beneath them. His lips were as delicate as the flowers I used to play in as a child. His teeth were the thorns on those flowers, inflicting a rush of pain and intensifying the pleasure he thrust upon me. I could have listened to his rough voice all day. I couldn't help but crave him as I sat in bed, picturing the next time we made love, and hoped I wouldn't have to wait as long.

I had to snap myself out of my own thoughts, and bravely stepped out of bed, motivated to do something other than grab food from a delivery guy or go to the toilet. I pulled on my silk dressing gown and strolled downstairs, avoiding my reflection in every mirror.

The house seemed normal, the same as before. It didn't change much when my life did. I almost didn't know why I'd contained myself in my room when I could have sprawled out across the whole house. It probably would have been tidier. Connor was notorious for not picking up after himself. In fact, it was one of his few pitfalls. At least he could count his lucky stars that he'd fallen in love with an organised, neat-freak who liked the place to look more like a new-build showroom than a warm home.

Without thinking, I started to pick up after Connor and knew exactly what to do with my first day as a free woman with no one at work to answer to—I was going to clean.

I started with taking his used plates and cups out and placed them neatly in the order I'd wash them on the kitchen counter. I then recycled the wrappers of his healthy snacks as I turned my nose up at the thought of mini cucumbers, and then hoovered. I spoke to my smart speaker like a friend and asked her to play me some music, which I blasted above the hum of the vacuum.

I loved music and whenever I listened to it, I always promised myself I'd listen to it more, but like all the promises I made myself, they always seemed to get buried under the responsibilities of life. Just like the promise I'd made myself growing up that I would quit work and travel the world, which I'd kept putting off —until now. I was already halfway there, maybe even three quarters. I just had to dig out my travel plans and wait for Connor to quit his job. Ideally, he'd give immediate notice but at worst, I hoped we'd only have to wait a month, and then we could go and live our lives in a vast world of beauty.

I switched off the hoover and started pulling things out of our messy drawer, counterproductive to the idea of cleaning the house.

There it was. A spiral bound, wanderlust journal, decorated with dried flowers and sequins. It was a mess, but it was my most treasured possession. I admit it could have been a lot prettier, but I'd started decorating the book fresh into high school, when all I wanted was to escape the strict parenting style of my father. He was never keen on my travelling gene. In fact, he was one of the reasons I'd waited all that time —him and Connor, of course.

I scanned the pages, reminding myself of travel plans that had taken the best part of my childhood to perfect. Pages were ripped out, pages were glued in, but it was my entire itinerary, obviously depending on the flights I was able to book—but it was all there; length of stay, hotel or hostel name, potential activities, tour operators and things to do to embrace the culture that was going to surround me. Everything.

Hours must have passed, and before I knew it, the sun had set behind the skyscrapers that sat on the horizon and Connor arrived home from a day shift. He came through the living room door and smiled before sitting down next to me and watching as I slowly turned the pages of my journal.

The washing up hadn't been done and the hoover wasn't put away. It was still plugged into the wall, but that didn't matter. Connor wasn't fazed by stuff like that, and even if he was, I could tell he was pleased I was out of bed and not wallowing in my own self-pity.

"Seeing this journal puts everything into perspective, doesn't it? I've quit my job. I still can't believe I have, but the world is my oyster. It was the right thing to do, wasn't it?" I said, my thumb stroking the open page.

"It was definitely the right decision. That place has been holding you back for so long, and as much as you love what you do, I can tell you've not been enjoying it as much. You used to come in excited about the cases you worked on. You barely shut up about them if I'm honest. But more recently, you'd mention them not out of excitement but to get it off your chest. Like it was a chore to speak about them, but you knew you needed to." His words rang truer than any spoken word I'd heard.

"You really do get me, don't you? You read me like a book."

He replied with a smirk and a kiss that lingered on my lips before he got up off the sofa and made his way to the kitchen. I didn't move. I continued to flick through the book and superimposed images of Connor and I onto the pictures I'd printed that had begun to fade.

Soon, I'm not going to need pictures. I'll have memories.

Connor came back in with two glasses of red wine, the liquid swirling around the bowls as he brought them in.

"I've wanted to sit with you and have wine for so long." He handed me a glass and sat as close as he possibly could. "Here's to not being passing ships for a while, and here's to you making the dreams you've had since you were a little girl a reality. I'm going to miss you so much, but I'll be waiting here for you when you get back. To the new Fleur." His glass raised as my face dropped.

"You'll miss me? You're coming with me," I said, not bothering to toast. What was there to toast to?

"How can I do that? I have work and my own things to sort out right here. I can't drop everything."

All those dreams I'd had of him being by my side as I travelled faded just like the pictures in front of me. All those times I'd put off going because the time wasn't right for him, when I could have gone. I resented myself waiting for the man I loved to follow my dreams. I resented him for making me feel I should wait, when it was clear now he had no intention of coming.

"I don't even know what to say." I was angry. I felt like throwing my travel journal across the room or hitting him repeatedly across the head with it, but the book had done nothing wrong.

"Look, sweetie, you need this. I don't want to hold you back. Go without me. You had this dream long before meeting me and our relationship." He tried to grab hold of my hand but I pulled away like a child having a tantrum. He was right. I had dreamt about travelling for nearly as long as I could remember, and I'd never wanted to share those dreams with anyone until I met Connor. That was the issue. He was never supposed to be the dream but he was, and it was difficult to shake off something that meant so much.

"And if I go, what about us?" I said the question through gritted teeth, as part of me didn't want to contemplate the answer he'd give, but I needed to know. I wasn't pleased at the thought of leaving the country without him for at least six months, but was I going to hold out on my dreams now, after giving up so much? Absolutely not.

"Well, I love you and I'm going to be here, waiting for you when you return, unless you meet a hunky Australian and decide to elope. Then I'll have to navigate London without you and I'll be homeless."

He laughed a little, and placed his hand on my leg. A move like that a couple of hours ago would have sent me wild. I didn't know if he was being sincere and he worried that I'd leave him. I wanted to reassure him, but also wanted to remind him that if it did happen, he'd understand exactly how Andrea felt. It wasn't going to happen, though. He was my everything.

"It would have to be the right Australian. They are too pretty, and you know I like my men a little rough around the edges." I gave him a wink, which must have turned Connor on like a light switch. He picked me up off the couch, giving me just enough time to place my journal on the coffee table and pick up my wine glass.

Connor carried me up the stairs and the wine spilled a little over his crisp white shirt that was about to be ripped from his body. Tonight was about pleasure. I was going to lap up everything he had to offer, every single inch, because I was about to leave him behind. I was pretty sure I was about to become a virgin again.

Chapter Eight

I was disappointed Connor wasn't going to be travelling with me, but he made up for it a little the night before and I had to look at the positives. It meant I didn't need to wait around in London longer than needed and I could get booking the next few months of my life up with the help of my trusty wanderlust journal.

First book, then pack.

My savings account was going to hate me.

Going back to The Netherlands was always going

to be the first place I'd visit. Hotel Iselmar was going to be my base in The Netherlands, only a short drive from the tulip fields and situated on a quaint port filled with gleaming yachts. That's how my grandma had described the hotel. It was where she'd had her wedding reception after marrying my grandpa. The hotel was luxurious, with a hot tub in the suite I was looking at. Although my trip was about being immersed into different cultures, I was not about to sacrifice my home comforts, not at first, anyway. I was determined to book the suite.

I entered the dates, only a few days away, and clicked to book.

Fully booked.

"Great," I said to myself sarcastically. "That's my travels off to a fantastic start."

The hotel was next available in two weeks, so I booked it. At least I'd have time with Connor before leaving.

Look on the bright side, Fleur.

My phone buzzed on the coffee table, alerting me to a phone call from my mother. My father never called, but he was always somewhere in the background, listening in and ready to pick apart anything that came out of my mouth.

I looked at my phone for a second, deciding

whether to continue avoiding them and the truth, or whether to face them head on. I chose a compromise.

"Hey, Mum, how are you? Say hi to Father from me," I said cheerfully, as if I'd not been avoiding them for the best part of a week.

"Oh, you answered. Are you not at work?" my mum chirped loudly down the phone. She hadn't quite grasped technology and would shout every time we spoke.

Gulp.

"No, Mum, I'm off for a while." I wasn't lying, just avoiding the truth.

"Oh splendid, for how long? You could come out to the Caribbean to see us. That would be lovely."

Of course they were on holiday. I could have guessed. A holiday with my parents with little to no escape? Usually I would have winced at the idea, but I had two weeks before I could check into the first destination of the rest of my life and a conversation to have with my father.

"Okay, you're on. Send me the details of where you're staying and I'll get a flight out." It made sense not to stick around, and I could be packed by tomorrow.

"Oh, Marcel, did you hear that? Our little girl is coming out to see us. It's been so..." The phone muffled as she spoke excitedly before putting the phone down.

It took my mum an hour to send over the hotel details. I probably could have worked out her location quicker from the photos of the pool she'd sent by accident by the time I received the address. In fact, I'd booked my accommodation and flights to Barbados in less time. I'd book the rest of my flights and accommodation for my trip while lounging by the pool in the scorching heat. Perfect.

I was leaving in two days. I had two days to tie up any loose ends, to get all my jabs for travelling abroad and then I had to pack. I didn't know what I was letting myself in for.

After booking in at a private clinic for my vaccinations, I tackled the packing debacle. I had always pictured being excited at this point in my journey, but I didn't know whether it was the masses of things I had to take with me and the stress of making it fit in my luggage allowance or the fact that I just wasn't excited to be going without Connor. I knew once I was on the plane I'd feel entirely different, and Connor had agreed to see me off at the airport.

My phone had already rung countless times within hours, all from my mum who'd call at the slightest of thoughts.

"Don't forget your toothbrush."

"Have you booked your transfer?"

"Are you sure Connor isn't able to join you?"

It was relentless.

This time, I was surprised to see Janine's name on my phone. I'd not spoken to her since walking out of work that day.

"Hello, stranger," I said, smiling down the phone. For what it was worth, Janine was one of the good guys and I already missed her company.

"Long time, no speak, Miss Abandoner. How are you doing?" She laughed.

"I'm actually doing good, you know. How's work? Falling apart without me already? Begging for me to come back? Is Walter crying into Steve's arse?" I cringed at the last comment but it came out of my mouth effortlessly like word vomit.

"Not quite, although it isn't the same without you. I just wanted to let you know that I've heard from Olly and he said Andrea has been to see him. She also wants to know if she can contact you in some way. Apparently, she'll be eternally grateful for all you did for her."

"That's great news she's been to see him. Of course, please pass my number on. I hope she's okay. Did he say how she looked?"

"I will do. He didn't, so that can only be a good thing."

"True. She's in good hands with Olly."

The phone went quiet for a few seconds. I didn't want our conversation to end, but Janine really had no obligation to talk to me anymore. Were we friends because I was her boss? Did she just say the office wasn't the same so I'd give her a good reference?

"So, what are you planning to do with yourself now you aren't working? Started your own legal firm yet?"

I sighed in relief.

"Ha, no. I'm actually in the middle of packing to go to Barbados tomorrow, and then the world is my oyster."

"Urgh, I hate oysters. You should come back here. If the world is your oyster you really won't like it." I could hear Janine giggling down the phone like a schoolgirl.

"You wish. Stay in touch, Janine. It's lovely to hear from you," I said with a smile beaming from ear to ear.

"You too."

After that call, I made a mental note to speak to Janine more and to not let leaving the firm get in the way of that. She was a good friend, and I had to count myself lucky to have her.

"So, this is goodbye." Connor spoke softly and held both of my hands as we stood amongst the crowds that filled the airport. I was about to check in and depart on the journey of the rest of my life—to find myself and all my missing pieces. I'd really hoped by the time we got to the airport that Connor would have changed his mind, packed a suitcase and travelled with me, even just for a little while. But that dream wasn't meant to be. Instead, I was going it alone and the excitement had started to creep in. No more waking up at the crack of dawn or being accountable to anyone or anything.

"It is. I really wish you were coming, but don't worry. I will still love you on the other side of the world, in fact, I'll probably love you even harder."

"Me too, sweetie. We'll talk every day, you know? It'll be just like when we were dating and we hadn't met each other." He looked me dead in the eyes, like he was excited to get back that spark we'd had when we first started seeing each other, like he was getting the old Fleur back.

"What, the constant texting and phone calls and spamming of images? You're gonna be sick of me."

"I could never be sick of you." His lips interlocked

with mine and in that moment, it didn't matter that we were making out in the middle of crowds of people, likely making everyone feel uncomfortable. At that moment, we were the only people who mattered.

"I'm going to miss you so much," I said, fighting back my tears. Was this what I wanted? Really? To leave and not look back for six months at least. To have a relationship only manageable through the power of technology? I'd have been lying if I said it was what I wanted, but I couldn't wait to be on that plane. I couldn't wait to meet new people and learn things about myself I'd never known. I couldn't wait to roll around in a field full of flowers.

"I'm going to miss you, too, more than you'll ever know." His muscled arms wrapped around me for the last time, so I soaked up his embrace. "Now, go check in or you'll miss your flight."

I heard what he said, but I couldn't help but remain in his arms for a couple of seconds longer. I pulled away from him with haste and mouthed the word bye to him, scared to talk because I knew my emotions would take control of my words and force an unrecognisable noise out in their place.

I didn't look back, because I was scared if I did, I would change my mind.

"Checking in?" The man spoke from behind the

counter, ready to weigh and send my baggage off to the aircraft.

"I am." I smiled and handed him my ticket and passport, but all I could think about was Connor. Was he still standing, watching me, waiting for me to go up through security to the departures lounge before leaving?

"Is your travel business or pleasure?"

"Pleasure," I said with certainty.

"Well, what better place than Barbados?" His hand flailed with excitement as he said my destination. I could tell he loved everything about his job. I couldn't have done it. I would have got envious of everyone fulfilling their travel dreams instead of me. Not anymore.

"You're so right. I just wish my boyfriend was coming with me."

His expression changed, and he withdrew a little. I made it awkward.

Go, Fleur!

"I can't magic your boyfriend here, but I can put you in first class. Consider it a consolation prize."

"Oh my gosh, seriously? That's incredible! Thank you so much." I pretty much ran from the counter after he checked me in, in case he changed his mind—

in case someone had a better sob story than me. I wondered if he thought my boyfriend had died?

I stepped onto the escalator and it carried me from check in towards security. I looked back to the place I'd stood with Connor, deciding to take one last look at him before I left the country because I couldn't change my mind now. I was on an escalator with people behind me, and I'd just got my ticket upgraded to first class.

He wasn't there.

People swarmed the last place we'd kissed like it meant nothing to them. It meant something to me.

I turned, facing forward and tried to not fall from the escalator while fighting to stop the tears from forming in my eyes, and began counting the days until I'd next see my man.

Chapter Nine

I'd never sat in first class before. I'd never had a reason to be on a plane for a long time. There I was, surrounded by people eloping, some maybe even going back to their home in Barbados. A lot of the men wore suits that looked like their tailors followed them around everywhere, altering their suits to fit them perfectly with each inhale and exhale.

I almost felt like I didn't belong in first class, sitting amongst the riches. Yes, I'd earned a decent salary and I'd saved my arse off for a long time, but this was on another level. Of course, I didn't complain and sipped on my Champagne quietly, minding my own business.

I put my headphones in and listened to a pre-made playlist, letting the music take me to far away places that were about to become reality.

I lay in a field of red and greens, looking up to the clouds and giving each one a name that suited their shape and size. I could hear my mummy and daddy talking on the chairs outside of the house. They were soaking up the rare sun in between the shadows cast by Jasper and Nelly, the clouds overhead.

I was glad it wasn't raining. It meant I got to be with the bugs and the flowers one last time before it was all gone.

As the days went by, Daddy kept on getting more and more serious. I didn't understand why, but I knew he mentioned his job a lot. It had something to do with money and that was all my parents seemed to talk about. I wished he told more jokes like he used to, or would chase me through the flower fields, pretending to be the tickle monster. Maybe he thought I was too old for that? I was five, after all, but I was never going to be too old for the tickle monster.

"Fleur, I've told you, you need to stop moving about in the flowers. You're going to ruin them all, and they're nearly ready to be sold."

BORINGGGG!

Grandma didn't care that I ruined her flowers. She said she had plenty and it would take me a whole month of running through her fields to ruin them all. She'd said by the time I'd done that I would have wasted away.

Daddy said we would leave this house by the middle of summer so Mummy had asked if there was anything I'd like to do before we left The Netherlands behind, so I told her I'd think about it. I wanted to stay, but apparently the UK was a better place to live. Apparently, London was the best place in the world. As much as I was excited to see Big Ben in real life and not in my books, I also wasn't ready to say goodbye to the windmills that made our town look so pretty.

I rolled back into the patch of flowers I was allowed to play in and continued watching the clouds. One the shape of a petal sat in the sky above me. It almost looked a blush pink colour if I squinted my eyes slightly against the rays of the sun. I called it Fleur.

One day, I was going to travel as far as that cloud, and we were going to be unstoppable.

The sun shone brighter than I'd ever seen it, with the heat caressing my skin and making me feel flustered the moment I stepped out of the airport. I slid into the private transfer that was waiting outside the airport. I even had a nice driver waiting for me in Arrivals with a sign like they did in movies.

The drive to Sandy Lane Hotel, one of the most luxurious hotels in Barbados, shone a light on my need to see the world. Back at home, I'd see style, grandeur and luxury each time I thought of Barbados, but that couldn't have been further from the truth. My taxi travelled past wooden huts that looked like they were about to topple over, poverty stricken towns and fields of nothing. If the sun hadn't been shining, it would have looked a bleak and miserable place. As the drive continued, we passed thriving wooden huts painted in quirky colours, the kind you saw on postcards. We drove past a huge shopping centre, one you could easily get lost in, and then along a road that lined the beach with hotels as far as the eye could see. That was Barbados. I almost felt a shred of guilt as I pulled up outside Sandy Lane Hotel, so I tipped the driver twenty percent, more than the usual expected ten.

"Petal, you're here!"

Of course they were waiting outside the resort for me to arrive.

"I am," I said after they'd stated the obvious. I gave them both a hug individually. Mum's hug was warm, and she lingered, not wanting to let go. My father's, on the other hand, was brief with a pat on my back. He even said he'd missed me, which was a surprise as I'd half expected a handshake.

They led me to a row of sun loungers that sat pool-side, and a waiter immediately presented the biggest cocktail I'd seen in my life, and I lived with a barman.

"Good flight?" Mum asked, always one for pleas-antries, which made up for the blunt nature of my father.

"Yep, not too bad. I slept for most of it." I grinned at the thought of seeing a petal shaped cloud and looked up to see if I could spot one. No such luck.

"It's not like you to have time off. Been fired?" There it was, a punch to my jugular. My mum slapped him playfully, but he lowered his sunglasses and waited for me to answer.

I took a deep breath. "No, I quit."

Both of them sat up in their sun loungers in shock. Luckily, they were both healthy otherwise I would have been dealing with two cardiac arrests.

"You quit? Why did you do that?" my mum asked, trying not to choke on a mouthful of her rum cocktail.

"I did. It's been a long time coming and you know how long I've been waiting to go and travel. Well, now's my chance. After this, I'm heading to The Netherlands, to the hotel where Grandma had her wedding reception, and then who knows? Wherever my book tells me, I guess."

My mum looked at my father, but he didn't say anything. He just looked at me. His sunglasses covered his eyes so I couldn't truly tell how he was feeling.

"Aren't you going to say something?" I asked him, wanting him to say all that was on his mind.

"I'm proud of you, Petal. You've worked your whole life helping people, earning a decent amount of money, but not once did you ever put yourself first, not that I've ever seen. For once, you're looking at following your dreams, and well, that makes your dad very proud." He'd never referred to himself as my dad, not once. It was always Father.

What he probably didn't realise was that I'd walked out and hadn't served my notice, and my legal career was likely to be over, but I was in no hurry to ruin a moment I'd longed for with my father.

"Awww, Dad. I love you. And you, Mum, so so much."

He didn't even correct me.

I sat around the pool, sipping a piña colada, and took in the view. A man walked past with his two children, a similar build to Connor. He was fairly attractive, and the greys in his hair glistened at the request of the sun.

"What an amazing parent... taking his children to a hotel like this one," I muttered under my breath. It took for me to be in my thirties until my parents had invited me to Barbados, mostly my own fault, although my parents had offered to pay for it. I'd politely declined.

Having children wasn't on my grown up to-do list, but if they were as well behaved as the children who walked by with their father, maybe I would have considered it.

Hey Connor. I've arrived at the resort safe and sound, and to my utmost surprise, my DAD is proud of me. I'll tell you more when we can speak over the phone when you're free, but I think I'm going to enjoy this break. Maybe those regular dinners with my parents aren't completely out of the window after all. I miss you x

I set my phone to the side of me and allowed the sun to consume me––all of me. Pale and pasty Fleur was going to be no more. I bathed in the sun for a few hours, the heat radiating against my skin and leaving that sun-kissed smell lingering in my nose. With each minute that passed, the more my chest released the pent up stress I had been unknowingly carrying for a long time. All the cases I'd dealt with, the arse-kissing and worrying I'd never be enough for my father.

That's great. I'm just heading to work for the evening so I'll speak to you tomorrow? I miss you more x

I locked my phone and pressed it close to my chest to feel that little bit closer to him, releasing a long sigh and attracting the attention of my father who had just taken a dip in the crisp blue water of the pool.

"Enjoying the sun, Petal?"

"Very much so," I said, inhaling the ocean air I could absolutely get used to.

"Good. I'm really glad you're here with us. I wish we'd known you were leaving your job. We could have planned to do more." His hand was on Mum's leg who was too occupied reading her book to even notice.

"Well, I actually only knew I was leaving a couple

of days ago. It's a long story really. Sorry I didn't tell you. I just didn't want you to be disappointed in me."

"A long story, how?" He ignored everything else.

"I took on a case but then my boss told me I shouldn't represent the client I wanted to. He wanted me to hear the opposition's point of view, who just so happened to be a friend of Walter's. He was an arsehole but made me feel like my gut could be wrong. And then both Connor and Walter told me I get too involved with my clients. I think I'd just had enough and it gave me the reason to quit I'd been waiting for all this time." I took a breath and then shut my eyes as I lay back down on my lounger, partly to avoid the sun shining directly in them but mostly to avoid eye contact. I fiddled with my thumbs nervously, waiting for his response.

"When have you ever let a man tell you what to do? When have you ever listened to a man and been bothered by what they have to say?"

"I've always cared what you think. I feel like that's the issue, though, because I'm so scared of disappointing you. I push you away because the further away from me you are, the less chance I have of disappointing you and not being the daughter you wanted."

For a second, there was silence, and even Mum

stopped reading her book, glancing at the both of us from behind it. My father shook his head and his eyebrows dropped with sadness.

"You are my daughter—a daughter I love and always will. I've raised you to be a force that could never be reckoned with. You have accomplished so much with very little help. I'm the luckiest father in the world and you could never disappoint me, Fleur." He got up from his lounger and placed himself next to me before wrapping his arms around me in an embrace I had craved ever since I was a child. As he held me, he continued to speak, and all I could do was nod along. "You're a grown woman, so you can go and live your life how you want to. You can even make mistakes, because making those mistakes will allow you to grow as a person. You're not a seed any more, you're a seedling, and when you get back from your travels, you'll be a blossoming flower and I'll be the proudest seedsman there ever was."

I pulled away to wipe my eyes. The pit of worry at the bottom of my stomach was there no more, knowing I had his blessing. My delay in going to The Netherlands had been a blessing in disguise, and I felt as close as I ever had to my parents.

That evening, I booked the next part of my travels, which included a tour of some countries in South East

Asia, including extra nights in Bangkok. I wrote down all the details in my journal as well as sending Connor the details for safety, but not before the tickle monster made an appearance in order to ascertain that I had the best father anyone could ask for.

Chapter
Ten

I 'd left Barbados with the love I felt for my parents burning brighter than it ever had. I had their blessing to travel with no feeling of guilt, and I was able to spread my wings and visit some of the most beautiful places in the world.

I landed at Amsterdam Schiphol Airport that wet April morning, flying for over twelve hours with a small layover in London. I contemplated going back home to see Connor, even for a few hours, but I changed my mind. Leaving him in London had been hard enough the first time, and I didn't think I'd be able to do it for a second.

The rain was different in The Netherlands than it was in the UK. Whenever it rained in London, the city would look dull and grey, but not in Amsterdam. The rain brought out people with brightly coloured umbrellas, and the colourful architecture of the buildings came to life.

"Can I have the red one, please?" I said to an elderly gentleman selling umbrellas on a side street, and paid with a five Euro note. My hair was already drenched, but remembering how much it used to rain here, I knew I was going to need one. Besides, I wanted to fit in. I was home, after all.

I smiled as I walked through the centre of the city--at people riding their bikes or shopping, and even at the dogs being walked by their owners riding their bikes and having the best time of their lives. I even smiled at things I couldn't get a response from, like the cup of coffee I sat with in a quaint coffee shop. I needed a break from lugging around my suitcase, but I couldn't check into my hotel for another few hours, so I wasn't about to pass up an opportunity to visit the city of canals--it wasn't going to be the last time either.

After finishing a romance novel on the flight over

the Atlantic, I cracked open another book by its spine and allowed each page to transport me to another world. For the first time, I didn't want to be anywhere else but The Netherlands, but not even the smell of freshly baked bread could make my stomach grumble enough to make me put the book down.

"More coffee, madam?" a young man asked as I quickly marked the page with my finger and looked at my watch.

"No, thank you, I'm fine. Just the bill please." I gave him a smile and his mouth widened, revealing the whitest and most beautiful smile I'd ever seen. He was young enough to have been my child if I'd wanted them, but I quickly shook off that thought and pulled out my travel journal to remind myself of the address of the hotel. I had written everything in there, including my hotel stay, travel plans and all my emergency contact information.

I placed down enough Euros to cover the coffee once the waiter had brought over the bill, added extra notes for a tip and started to pack away my things.

"You are beautiful, ja," he said, his accent forcing goosebumps to appear on my arms and shivers to run to the bottom of my spine.

"That's very kind." I blushed as much as I flustered, grabbing my suitcase and bumped into furniture in my haste on my way out of the coffee shop.

I hadn't realised how uncomfortable receiving compliments made me––I hadn't had a problem like that in the past; I'd even go as far as saying I'd welcomed them. I'd fallen out of love with myself, but I hoped this trip would rectify that.

I hailed a taxi, still looking hot and bothered, but settled in the leather seats of the taxi en route to my hotel. I flicked through images of my grandparents' wedding and reception on my phone, trying to contain my excitement to see how picture perfect it was. I only had the photos and no memory of the day as it had happened long before I was born, but I could still hear my grandma's delicate voice describing how her lace dress had lifted so effortlessly in the coastal breeze.

She was the most beautiful bride. I only hoped I'd look half as beautiful on my wedding day––whenever that would happen.

Arrived safely at my hotel. The Netherlands is so beautiful. I wish you were here to see it for yourself. These two weeks have been so weird not having you by my side. Maybe we could speak on the phone soon? I love you x

I sent a quick text to Connor as the taxi pulled up next to the breathtaking Hotel Iselmar. It was surrounded by canals, gleaming white sail boats and luscious greenery. The pictures from all those years ago did it no justice, and it was clear the hotel had undergone a spruce up in the last few years.

I inhaled a deep breath of fresh sea air and wheeled my suitcase into the hotel.

My phone rang as I was checking into my suite, and with a glance to make sure it wasn't Connor, I placed it back in my bag.

"Would you like help to your suite, miss?" an elderly lady said, already clicking her fingers to a bell boy on standby. I had no choice.

"Thank you. That would be great."

I swished up along a corridor once we got out of the lift. The bell boy didn't bother making small talk, and I was quite happy looking at all the hand-painted portraits that lined the hallway to my room.

As soon as the door opened, I thanked the young lad who had carried my suitcase with a small tip. My mouth opened as I looked across the large room to a king size bed with a modern light illuminating underneath as well as a jacuzzi sat prominently in the centre of the room. I jumped onto the bed, my aching muscles comforted by the soft duvet I sank into. I gazed at the small LED lights that were dotted above the bed like glistening stars in the night sky.

My phone started to ring once more, so I leapt across the room to where I'd left my bag to answer the call from a Dutch number.

"Hello, Fleur speaking," I said politely. I may have quit my job but I would never lose my phone voice.

"Madame, it's Dann. From the coffee shop."

"Hello?" I questioned. Thankfully, he was on the phone and couldn't see my confusion.

"You left your journal on the table––your travel journal. I 'ave it for you."

"Oh my gosh, thank you. I must have left it there by accident."

No shit, Sherlock. He knows that.

I rolled my eyes at myself.

"I will keep it safe. You can come and collect, ja," he said as I pictured his bright smile through the phone. Just hearing him speak that little Dutch at the end brought so many childhood memories back to the forefront of my mind.

"I will be there as soon as I can. Thank you."

My taxi pulled up to the coffee shop and I hopped out, no longer having to worry about the rain battering against me. I opened the door and immediately spotted Dann amongst his colleagues. He was the youngest, and prettiest—almost too pretty. I threw him a smile as he finished taking a customer's order and then grabbed my journal from behind the bar.

I stood awkwardly near the doorway, getting in everyone's way as I waited for him. He strolled over, his posture oozing a confidence I only wished I possessed.

"Your journal, Fleur." I wondered how he knew my name, but I remembered introducing myself.

"Thank you so much for keeping it safe. You have no idea how much this journal means to me." This book meant the world to me, if only inanimate objects knew that. If only I could tell it to not leave my sight ever again after having to take an hour's taxi journey in the pouring rain.

"Maybe you can tell me about your travel plans over a drink?" His voice was smooth. A younger version of me would have been weak at the knees for him if I hadn't been so involved in my studies and my career.

"That sounds lovely, but I'm in a relationship, I'm sorry." I said as my cheeks grew rosier by the second. I still hadn't heard from Connor since my last text but I didn't need to worry. He was always working. I knew that he'd text me on his break or after his shift like he always did.

"Ah, well if you change your mind..." He pulled his

order pad from his pocket and scribbled his name and phone number across the page.

I shook my head and then smiled, taking the number and placing it in my bag––anything for an easy life. Reunited with my travel journal, I embraced the book to my chest as I walked out of the coffee shop to grab a taxi to my hotel, making sure not to let it out of my sight.

Chapter Eleven

The following morning started out like any other I'd had on my travels. I woke up relaxed, without any stress, made a hot drink and then got back into bed to stretch out my aches and pains from having too much sleep. I grabbed my travel journal to look at my itinerary for the day and checked my phone for the usual text message I'd receive off Connor.

Nothing. Not one text. Not one goodnight. Not one kiss.

I called his phone but it went straight to voicemail.

Worry set up residence in the pit of my stomach. A couple of hours in between messages was normal for us, but not a day. Never a day.

I flicked through a few pages in my journal to see the many things I could do while visiting The Netherlands: Rijksmuseum, Anne Frank's house or heading to the biggest amusement park. I'd not been to an amusement park since I was a child. In fact, I'd not let my hair down like that for a while either, but none of those could measure up to visiting my first home and my grandma's flower fields.

I packed up my bag after allowing my coffee to work its magic, along with a polaroid camera to have instant printed pictures to journal along the way. The book wasn't just an itinerary; it was a place I could go after my travels to relive all the beautiful memories I made along the way.

It had only been one full day since seeing my parents and I already felt a smidge of loneliness. Not hearing back from Connor wasn't helping the feeling either. That was going to change as I'd be in South East Asia with a group of people in just under a week. And those people were going to want the same as me-- experiences of a lifetime.

I set out that morning and embraced the warm sun

as a welcome change from the rain. I took a long stroll down towards but not as far as Emmeloord, the closest town to where we'd lived and where we'd done all our shopping.

Not even half an hour into my walk, down the straightest road ever, I came across bright red and sunshine yellow tulips. April was the best time to see the flowers, with the tulips in full bloom. I walked along a path but crossed the road onto a grassy embankment to take photos of their beauty.

Another hour seemed to pass by in a flash and I found myself walking up a narrow, one track road that ran alongside my childhood home. My grandparents' home. Their flower fields.

I was overwhelmed and sat on the edge of the road looking at the reds, whites and yellows of the flowers that swayed slightly in the light breeze. It was the most beautiful day. Perfect.

I located the place where I'd played as a child, the section of the flower field where I was allowed to lie down and play with the bugs. Where it didn't matter if I ruined the flowers. The tulips were blooming just as bright as anywhere else on the field. You wouldn't have known it was once as bare as the flower fields in October.

I looked around and enjoyed the silence. There was

not a single car on the drive or on the road, which seemed to go on for miles. There was nothing around me––nobody, not even the tweeting of birds filled my ears. I paced a little on the roadside, constantly looking in different directions until I built up enough courage to step onto their land and into their flower field. I was overcome with emotions: nervous to stand where I'd once stood as a child, but also nervous to be trespassing. Something Little Miss Good Girl Fleur would have never done.

It used to be my home, but I had no right to be there.

I stood, feeling overwhelmed that I'd finally managed to go back to the place I'd always said I would. Sad at the thought of not being able to hear my grandma's voice shout across the field, just like she always had when my tea was ready.

I looked up to a few clouds that had started to appear in the sky and smiled. I tried my best to give them appropriate names, finding it difficult without the imagination I'd had as a child.

A loud ring came from my bag, startling me in the midst of the silence where I stood in the middle of someone else's field, trying my best not to step on any of the flowers.

Connor.

"Hey, Connor, are you okay?" I said immediately, giving him no chance to speak first.

"Hey, yeah, I'm fine…"

"That's good. I was worried about you because you hadn't messaged, but anyway. I'm glad you've called. Guess where I am?" I asked with a huge grin, breathing in the floral air that surrounded me.

"I've no idea," he said, his words lacklustre.

"What's up with you? You don't seem like yourself." I twiddled with my thumbs as I waited for his response. There was a long pause and nothing but his breath echoed down the phone.

"Fleur." I waited, not answering my name. "I can't do this anymore."

Air caught at the back of my throat, getting larger and larger each time I tried to respond but couldn't, forming a lump that wouldn't go away. My mind hazed over just as clouds covered the sun that had bathed me all day.

"What?" I wanted to say more but I couldn't. I didn't understand.

"I can't be with you anymore, not like this. Not seeing you for two weeks while you were in Barbados has given me time to think."

"Think about what? Is this why you didn't come with me?" Tears ran down my throat instead of down my cheeks and my body ached at everything he said.

"One of the reasons. Admit it, Fleur, we've not been right for a long time, and this time apart has done us both good. We need to move on."

"Move on? Move on!" I yelled, my voice carrying across the fields into nothing. I started pacing, carelessly stepping on the tulips that surrounded me. I lifted my feet to find a red tulip in pieces on the floor, looking as battered as my heart felt as it thumped twice as fast in my chest. "I'll come home. We can sort this out." I tried to reason with him. I tried to save us because I wanted to understand and I couldn't come to terms with all he had to say.

"I won't let you do that. This is not a reason for you to come home. You've stopped yourself travelling for so long. Now you have one less reason to come home." He was trying to be nice but God, it hurt-- like holding onto a single rose with a stem full of thorns. "I've already moved my things out and I've posted my key through the letter box. I'm sorry, Fleur, but I'm done."

The phone went silent and I fell to the floor as I grieved our relationship, sitting on the flowers that had once brought me so much joy. I didn't have a chance to get angry at him, something I'd probably be grateful for one day, because I would not have been in control of everything I'd have said.

My favourite place in the world was now laced with pain. I couldn't bear to sit and look at the flowers anymore––to sit and pretend that my life was okay watching bugs or naming the clouds. I wasn't okay.

I put my phone back into my bag, catching a glimpse of Dann's name and phone number as my mind taunted me.

"I'm in a relationship."

Ha. You could have gone on the date with the young lad. Connor's probably already seeing someone else. He's even moved his things out.

I shook my head, ridding the thoughts from my mind.

I picked myself up and began to walk with what little energy I had left, which seemed to diminish each time a tear rolled down my cheek. I made sure to kick a few tulips on my way off the farm as my feet ran across the ground. I was angry. Broken.

I walked along the grassy embankment back towards my hotel. I hadn't wanted to go back there. I didn't want to be anywhere nor did I want to be by myself, but I had nowhere else to go. I must have been walking for an hour but I couldn't have been sure. I caught a glimpse of a man looking down to his field of flowers, some blooming bright but others wilted and trodden.

Stupid damn flowers.

"Ga van mijn bloemen af, kanker!" I heard him shout but I continued to walk, flailing one of my hands above my head to acknowledge him. "Get off, toerist!" he persisted, still shouting at me until I had no choice but to retaliate.

"I'm not on your fucking flowers and I'm not a tourist!" I screamed at him, my torso turning to face him, only to see him walking towards me. The closer he got, the more I could see the outline of his pecs through his tight white vest top. The closer he got, the more I could see his expression--his eyebrows pointed with anger but his eyes were as sad as mine. He stood towering over me, close enough for his masculine scent to dance in my nostrils.

"I wasn't in your flowers," I said, trying to hold back my tears, trying to be the powerful Fleur I used to be.

He looked down at me--he must've been about a foot taller than me. He gazed into my eyes and I looked into his. Adrenalin must have been fuelling me, because the Fleur I'd become wouldn't have looked this hunk square in the face for long. She would have run.

"You've been crying?" His voice was softer than before. I nodded. "Why are you walking by yourself?"

"It's a long story," I said, as I looked down and broke eye contact with him. I saw his filthy hand twitch by his side, like he wanted to comfort me. Like he wanted to touch me. They were covered in soil from tending to his flowers. The field that someone had clearly run through, probably youths. I wouldn't dare tell him I'd done the same just south of his farm.

"Coffee?" he asked.

I probably shouldn't have nodded. I probably shouldn't have walked into a stranger's home after he'd just been shouting at me, but the thought of sitting by myself in my hotel room was more depressing than anything else I could think of.

I sat holding on to my freshly poured coffee as he pulled up a chair next to me.

"Levi," he said simply.

"Fleur."

"You're Dutch?"

"I am, well, kind of. I used to live a couple of miles away from here as a child. My grandparents owned a tulip farm just like yours. I was here visiting."

"You're crying because you miss them?" he asked, as his hand moved once more, this time a little closer to mine wrapped around the coffee mug.

"Amongst other things."

It was good to get everything off my chest, to talk about the phone call from Connor that had come out of the blue. Levi listened to each and every word of mine, nodding and humming in response.

"Sorry for crying. I must look horrendous right now," I said, sniffing through some tears.

"This Connor is a fool. You are beautiful. Heel mooi." I tried to look away but he wouldn't let me. His eyes burnt deep into mine and my skin felt as if it was on fire the moment he finally placed his hand on mine.

For a second, my world stopped.

For a minute, my world was put to rights, until I saw his silver wedding ring glisten underneath his kitchen spotlights.

Chapter Twelve

"Would you like to see my travel journal?" I pulled away from his touch and reached into my bag, with all the will in the world to change the subject.

I picked out my journal and flicked to my upcoming break in South East Asia. I talked Levi through my itinerary and occasionally glanced at his hand to where his wedding ring sat on his finger.

I wondered who I'd become without Connor in my life, despite the fact the thought made me squeamish. Would I be flirty? Fun and reckless without a care in the world? I knew my life would go on, as much as I couldn't bear the thought of living without Connor. And yet, Levi sat with his eyes glistening in front of me, wanting to initiate something. A kiss or maybe more. I didn't know what the new Fleur would bring to the table, but I knew for certain that I wasn't about to stand in the way of a married couple. I'd seen a lot of hurt during my time as a solicitor. Andrea was a perfect example of that, and I was not about to be the type of person to cause that pain.

"So, from Thailand, I'll be going to Cambodia, Vietnam and Laos," I said, showing him the pictures I'd printed long ago. He was interested in my plans, I could tell. He asked questions about my travels and about me.

Maybe that was the issue with Connor?

Maybe he'd never had the desire to come with me.

Maybe he thought my dream was never going to be a reality.

"What's this place? It looks like a fairy tale." His finger ran across an image of the full moon lantern festival in Hoi An, Vietnam. Once a month, they turned off all the fluorescent lights at eight in the evening and then floated multicoloured lanterns down the river.

"I honestly can't wait to see the city glow. It will be so beautiful. So romantic." I accidentally looked up, making eye contact, and I couldn't tear myself away. Not with how he was looking at me.

His head moved closer to mine––his lips even closer. His pupils seemed so deep I could have fallen into them. The power his one look held over me was unexpected, and as much as I really didn't want to kiss him, I also really did.

His mouth met mine and my bottom lip shook underneath his until his rough hand caressed the back of my neck. His kiss was soft, passionate, like he wanted each of his kisses to soothe the pain I felt. It was working. His lips were delicate but as his hand firmly pressed against my neck, my legs clasped around his as I craved more of him.

Until I stopped.

I'd given myself freely to him, but in doing so, I'd forgotten my morals.

I pulled away even though I craved more. More of him. More of how he made me feel.

"But, you're married." My head nodded to the wedding ring that sat firmly on his finger. It had been there a long time, almost as if his finger had moulded to its shape around it.

He understood and pushed back into his seat before getting up and pacing around his kitchen.

"I am not married," he said as sadness scratched at his voice. "Would you like another cup of coffee?"

I nodded and watched him pour me another from the cafetière while I waited for him to elaborate, but nothing.

"I'm sorry." The truth was that I didn't need him to elaborate. In my experience, there were only three reasons why he'd still be wearing his ring: He couldn't get it off, he hadn't wanted to separate or his wife had passed. Looking around his home and feeling his kiss, one he planted on me in his very own home, I figured it was the latter. Or he was lying, but my gut told me he wasn't.

"You don't need to be sorry," he said as he continued to pace around the kitchen. "She died a few years ago. It was, how do you say? Slaan en rennen."

"Hit and run?" He nodded.

"Yes. The driver never stopped." When he let me, I could see the hurt in his eyes. I wanted to take his pain away, like just being in his company was doing for me.

Levi ran his hands through his dirty blond hair that fell perfectly back into place, and then his hands hit the kitchen counter in an almighty rage. The noise startled me, making me inch my chair backwards and bring me to the realisation that I was still in a stranger's house--an angry, emotional, caring and loving, stranger's house.

"I think it's probably best if I go. I'm sorry." I stood up and picked up my bag, about to put my travel journal away when he spun me around on my feet. At first, I gasped in shock as his hand wrapped around my waist. Before long, I admitted defeat and sank into his hand that kept me standing, placed at the base of my spine.

"No, don't go. Please." His request was simple and I obliged.

His other hand wrapped itself perfectly around the back of my neck and sat like it was meant to be there and nowhere else. With each second that went by, I surrendered to him, melting into each touch. Each word. Each smile.

"You are so beautiful, Fleur. Even more beautiful than my tulips."

His lips met mine, as delicate as petals on a flower, and for a while, I was okay with them brushing against mine. His teeth were sharp, like the thorns you'd find on a single rose. I'd usually avoid allowing the thorns to touch me, but the pain his bite induced felt so good. The way they pulled at my bottom lip made me beg for mercy and yet still somehow I wanted more.

Pleasure fluttered and flew through my body, making me tingle in places he hadn't yet touched. I wished for the way he made me feel to never end––for his touch to run up and down my body forever. I wouldn't get anything done and I wouldn't be able to travel the world, but as I quivered under his breath, I accepted that fate with open arms.

I wanted to rip off his vest top but he'd taken it off before I was given the chance. My hand fell from his chest, running down each of his abs and his muscles shaped into a perfect V. I had to stop myself from letting out a moan.

He picked me up and I wrapped my legs around his torso as he walked me into his bedroom.

He was everything.

It was everything––everything I needed and didn't know it. Not once did I think about Connor. He didn't let me.

Not until I woke in his bed a few hours later to nothing but a pile of duvets and his musky smell that lingered along with an ache that wouldn't go away at the thought of Connor. It hadn't been a day since he'd broken my heart and I'd already tried to patch it up temporarily. It wasn't like me. I was the type of woman to cry in my room for days, not jump into bed with a handsome stranger just minutes after he'd allowed my world to start to spin again.

I hopped out of his bed, pulling on clothes while trying to hide my nude body with his duvet in case Levi suddenly reappeared from the bare space he'd left in his bed. It wasn't as easy as it looked in the movies. I then made my way through to the kitchen, following the light noises as he cleaned. My bag was placed tidy, my travel journal sitting closed next to it, and two plates were laid on the table waiting to be graced with food.

"Oh great, you're up. I'm making food if you want?" I wanted to say yes because I knew I'd struggle to say no, but truthfully, I couldn't eat. Not with the regret that made my stomach turn. I didn't regret him. How could I? He was someone I'd remember forever. But, I did feel guilty for giving myself to him so quickly and so freely after Connor, because I had acted so out of character.

"No, I'm okay. I best go," I said as I edged my way towards the kitchen table.

"Oh, okay. Can I see you again?" I nodded to his question, but gave him no verbal clarification of whether he and I would be seeing each other again. I was a woman of my word, so I couldn't lie.

Looking at his abs that sat just above the waistband of his trousers and remembering how he'd made me feel a few hours ago, of course I wanted to see him again, but I was leaving in a few days to go to South East Asia. I wasn't going to let a guy hold me back anymore, not like I'd allowed to happen for so long.

I walked over to him and stood a few inches away —close enough for our breath to intertwine and long enough to capture a mental image of him. Someone I never wanted to forget. The guy who saved me on the worst day of my life.

I left a sweet kiss on his left cheek and then picked up my bag, not forgetting my journal this time, and walked out into the fresh evening air.

That's it, Fleur, you're back to your typical self-- rushing off and pushing people away who could one day really care about you.

Chapter Thirteen

Less than a week later, I arrived in Bangkok. I had gone days without seeing or speaking to Levi, despite the fact that he'd written his phone number in my travel journal. I'd spent days being angry with Connor and ignoring his pitiful texts that came through to check if I was okay. He was messaging out of guilt, but I took far too much joy in not replying out of spite for the way he'd treated me. I deserved better than being the woman he could just break up with over a phone call after all those years. I deserved better than him.

I walked out of the five-star hotel with my travel journal in hand, a large rucksack on my back, and a whole lot of excitement as I made my way to the meeting point for the tour I was joining. I wondered who I'd meet and if they'd become friends, since the only real friends I had were Janine and now Andrea. She hadn't stopped messaging me. I knew she was probably lonely, adapting to a life that didn't include her husband. It was no chore to text her; we had lots in common after all. We both had backstabbing ex-partners who would go to the ends of the earth to ruin our lives. *Sigh*. Connor was right, though. I didn't have many friends, so I was eager to make some new ones.

I pictured visiting places I'd dreamed about for so long––laughing, smiling, taking photos and feeling free. I knew that not even my mind could have conjured up a picture of how incredible these places were.

As I wandered the streets, I had to fight through crowds of people and couldn't stop to take a look at my surroundings without getting in someone's way, so my steps remained small and consistent as I walked in time with the crowds ahead. My ears stung at the noise that swept the streets. I used to think London was busy, with nowhere to catch your breath, but being in Bangkok made London feel like the countryside.

I walked into the bar that sat under Mad Monkey Hostel to meet the group in person after chatting to them a little via Whatsapp. None of us had stayed at the hostel prior to that night and we didn't know what to expect. However, according to our organiser it was the place to be for backpackers. Completely hip and very cheap. I didn't feel it was necessary to tell them I'd just spent the night sipping and enjoying Champagne in a jacuzzi bath.

The bar had bright orange neon lighting and a swimming pool, with backpackers already splashing around while holding onto their beers, underneath the multicoloured bunting that hung over the pool. If the hostel rooms were anything like the bar, we were going to be alright.

"Stop shaking my boobs! People are looking," a young female said as her friend grabbed hold of them.

"They aren't your boobs. They're mine!" her friend piped up. "You didn't mind me playing with them last night."

Oh God. Please don't be on my tour. Please don't be on my tour.

That was when the organiser came out of the toilet

with the orange flag he'd attached to his backpack so we'd know it was him.

"Keira. Courtney. Another drink?" he asked, shouting over to the girls. Their response was a thumbs up.

They were on my tour. Two rowdy, sexual beings. I couldn't have been more of an opposite.

"Hey, Lee. It's Fleur." I introduced myself and shook his hand, but he immediately kissed me on both cheeks before pulling himself away from the bar with the drinks in his hands.

"Hi, Fleur, great to finally meet you. This is Keira." He pointed to the girl who had been shaking her girlfriend's boobs not a few minutes ago. I smiled and put my hand out but was pulled into a seat next to her and given a hug.

"And this is Courtney," Keira said as she placed her hand on her girlfriend's knee. A nice change to the pair of boobs they'd just been all over. I waved to her while Keira sat in between us.

"So lovely to meet you both. Where are you guys from?" I asked, trying to make small talk in between looking at the entrance of the pub each time someone else walked in--hoping, praying, the others would be arriving soon.

"America. We met a few years back on a tour of

Australia and fell for each other. Now we live together in Seattle and we thought we would relive the magic of the first time we met," Courtney said, her accent more southern than Kiera's.

"That's so cute," I said sincerely, holding back the jealousy that bubbled in my throat.

"You're British, aren't you?" Keira asked just as Lee brought a drink over for me.

"I am. Well, I live in London but I'm originally from The Netherlands."

"Cool. That's where they've got those awesome windmills, right?" Keira asked, as had ninety percent of the people I'd met the minute I'd told them I was from The Netherlands.

"Among many other things, yes. I was visiting a couple of days ago. It was my first time back there since being a young child."

"That sounds amazing," Courtney said, holding up her glass. "Here's to many more memories. Cheers!"

Our glasses clinked together and before long, mine was empty. I needed the Dutch courage that was hidden deep inside me.

"Everyone, this is Austin. He's joining us on our travels, too." Lee introduced him as a young man joined us at the table.

"Hi, how are you guys?" Austin said as he held out his hand for me to shake.

"Fleur," I said as my hand met his.

I could tell from his accent he was British, and so could the others.

"Boooo! Not another one from England." Kiera laughed at herself with everyone else following. She was so bubbly and infectious I couldn't help but laugh along. Maybe it was the drink talking, or maybe I was warming to her.

"Where in the UK are you from?" I asked Austin as a pint of beer quickly vanished down his throat in an attempt to catch us all up.

"Oxford, you?"

"London. I was going to go to university there but I ended up in Cambridge instead."

"Ouch, that hurts." He winked as he ruffled his hair to naturally fall as curtains. "Oxford is a much better university."

"Maybe now, but it wasn't better when I applied to do my law degree."

"Oh yeah, and when was that? A couple of years ago?"

"I'm going to be showing my age now, but I graduated as a qualified solicitor about nine years ago." The others listened in, their heads following our conversation like a ball in a game of tennis.

"You don't look old enough for that to be the case."

"What a charmer." I took his compliment without thinking about it––without my cheeks blushing a bright shade of red. Again, it was likely to have been the drink.

An hour or so later, the last member of our tour walked through to where we were sitting. Her name was Paige and she was the youngest of us all. At only nineteen years old, she had travelled to meet us all the way from New Zealand. I worried at first, in my own head, about being the oldest of the group, but I quickly reminded myself that my age didn't define me. I could have just as much fun as the others––I was going to.

She sat next to Austin and his attention quickly turned to her. She was beautiful, after all––the whitest of hair and her skin as golden as the sands of the Sahara.

I listened into their conversations, sipping my drink and feeling a little out of my comfort zone. I could talk to anyone. I would have even called myself confident, but I was conscious they wouldn't like me. I'd gone my whole life caring too much for people around me, and had wanted them to care for me.

Tonight, we'd be sleeping in the same place. Tomorrow, we'd be spending the whole day together. For the next few weeks, they were my people. They had to be, otherwise my dream trip would quickly become a living nightmare.

I woke up and stretched as much as I could in the smallest bed I'd ever slept in. I was sure my crib as a child had been bigger. It turned out the rooms weren't a patch on the bar downstairs. However, it was nice to fall asleep to the sound of my newly found friends' voices. Austin and Keira were the ones who always kept the conversation flowing and they always found a reason to include me. I already felt a sense of belonging with them and felt far from lonely. The sun was shining bright and the heat was already a humid high of twenty-five degrees celsius. Staying at the hostel and lounging in and around the pool was an easy decision. The water was cool and the view was something of a people-watcher's dream. I was able to sip my coffee at the edge of the pool and watch as people walked past or arrived at the hostel.

"Paige," I yelled, waving like a crazy person as she strolled into the bar from upstairs. I wished for my youth back only to sleep as long as her again.

"Hi, Fleur," she said, elongating her words. "How did you sleep?"

"So so, it could have been worse. I'm not missing my home comforts just yet. You?"

"I slept like a log. Do you mind if I join you in the pool?"

"Not at all." She pulled off her loose t-shirt to reveal a white bathing suit underneath. Her body was ridiculous, almost unobtainable. I blamed her youthful metabolism.

"I hate you," I said playfully, looking down at my body. I was practically watching the clock and waiting for my body to sag with age.

"Why? What have I done?"

"You're stunning and I hate you for it." I laughed so she cannon balled into the pool to cover me with water. If I hadn't looked too bad before that, my wet rat look certainly would have sealed that deal.

I wiped my eyes free from the chlorine while I watched a young Thai man pull up on a motorcycle and deliver a package to the hostel check in desk. One down side of travelling in South East Asia was that I couldn't understand or decipher what everyone was saying like I could in The Netherlands.

The man who had been standing behind the desk since I'd arrived the day before walked up to me. "Fleur, this came for you."

A package? For me?

There was nothing on the brown packaging to say who it was from, and it only had my name written in beautiful calligraphy. I carefully tore open the packaging to find a single flower with a handwritten note attached with some string. It was a rose, red in colour, and its stem held on to the most petals I'd ever seen on a flower.

Struggling to catch my breath without you,
Fleur x

"Oooooh, someone's got a secret admirer. Tell me more," Paige said, swimming closer and leaning against the edge of the pool ready to be filled in.

I placed the rose on the poolside and studied the note.

It was Connor. A pathetic attempt at an apology.

I wondered what had happened for him to change his mind. I internally laughed at the thought of him wondering how to pay his bills without me or coping with the stress of moving house. That was even if he had left our house. My house. I'd taken his word for it.

"It's clearly from my ex-boyfriend. He broke up with me not even a week ago and it seems like he's already realised he made a mistake."

"How do you know it's from him?"

"Who else would it be? Besides, we always used to put one kiss on all of our messages. It's definitely him."

"Are you going to talk to him?"

Part of me wanted to think about whether I would, but he didn't deserve a text from me, let alone a phone call, and thankfully we were over five thousand miles away from each other.

"Nah. He really hurt me. It's gonna take a lot more than a single rose for me to consider giving him any more of my time."

Chapter Fourteen

"He was so cute. I wish I could have taken him home," Courtney said as we walked towards Khao San Road. We'd been to a Thai cooking class and made pad thai, which we were able to eat afterwards. Mine was delicious although I was scrutinised by the rest of the group for adding prawn and not chicken to mine.

It didn't take long for the whole class to know about the rose and note that had been delivered to our hostel, not when it came to my group of friends. They spread the gossip so quickly across the room it was like wildfire. I wasn't used to being the topic of conversation, not when I'd spent my life learning and practising ways of defending those around me and talking about them instead. However, all those late nights and fast food orders came in handy when it came to our cooking class, because not knowing how to cook was the perfect excuse to change the subject. I found that out by chopping an onion the wrong way. Who knew there was a wrong way to chop an onion?

"I think border control may stop you the moment you tell them you're taking an elderly Thai man home because he is cute." I laughed.

We could barely hear each other as we were sardined in between the crowds. My senses seemed to overload as we walked past different restaurants and bars, with the smell of spices lingering in my nose. I was thankful for that, because with the amount of people surrounding me, someone was bound to smell of sweat.

The streets echoed with the voices of those trying to sell things to backpackers and lit up by huge billboards and neon lighting. We were pulled into bar after bar, lured in by their offers and promises of free drinks. We didn't mind where we ended up as long as we were together. Our motto for the trip was 'everything that happens, good and bad, is part of the experience', something that I was going to embrace.

"Oh my God, let's all get matching tattoos!" Keira said, and I instantly laughed at her excitement. She was being serious.

"Oh no. Na-ah. No way. You hear stories about getting tattoos on the side of streets. Nope."

"Come on, remember our motto. Please," Keira said, elongating her words persuasively.

"It's funny how that didn't apply when I was trying to encourage you all to eat a prawn during our cooking class."

"The motto doesn't apply to fish related things," Paige spoke out, just as passionate about not eating fish as she was eager to get matching tattoos.

"I disagree. And look at that... There just so happens to be a very delicious looking food stall opposite that sells fish. I'll get a tattoo if you all buy and eat a prawn."

Objection roared from the group, but I stood assertively, standing my ground. I was acting like all of their mothers, trying to lure them into eating their greens before allowing them the television remote.

"Fine." Kiera went off in a huff to buy four king prawns, bringing them back to the group. "Eat these."

The rest of the gang questioned her while I smugly

looked at them all. Kiera's face turned smug back at me.

"Why are you looking like that? They've not eaten the prawns yet and neither have you."

Keira bit into the prawn, swallowing it without chewing and within seconds it had disappeared down her gullet.

"Because, Fleur, you've agreed to get a tattoo if we all eat a prawn, yet you have no idea what the tattoo is going to be of."

It was at that moment, I knew I'd messed up. I'd underestimated her just like I'd been underestimated far too many times. I should have recognised Kiera for who she was: a force to be reckoned with. She and I weren't too dissimilar after all.

I watched them, one by one, eat the prawns. Some put on a brave face and others shuddered with each chew. Whatever the tattoo was of, their faces had to have been worth it.

"Five tattoos please. We'd like 5 penises, all on our wrists."

"Whoa. No. I'm a solicitor. I *was* anyway. I can't have a dick on my wrist."

"Everything that happens, good and bad, is part of the experience," they all hummed together, with some of them clapping along.

"What about Lee? He's not here." I tried to think of anything to avoid the inevitable.

"He's our tour guide. He doesn't count." Paige then giggled and grabbed my hand, forcing me closer to the tattoo shop and the lights that poured from the signage to make it stand out on the busy street.

"Do you not have anything to say about this?" I looked to Austin, hoping he'd rebel against them and not want a penis to be permanently marked onto his skin."

"Oh, baby, having this tattoo will be more than worth it after your reaction. Besides, I'm gonna need the penis to tie in with the boob tattoo I got on my other wrist yesterday with the lesbians." They both smiled and didn't flinch at his lesbian comment. Well, they were lesbians, so it wasn't really an insult. It seemed they'd formed a little tattoo club without Paige and me knowing.

Unbelievable.

"Fine. Everything that happens, good and all the absolutely rotten bad tattoos are part of the experience," I said sulking, and held out my wrist before I could change my mind.

I watched as the ink bled into my skin, contemplating if one day I'd be able to get the penis turned into a flower, or if I'd ever want to get rid of the tattoo and memories of this crazy bunch.

———

One overnight bus later and we arrived in Cambodia at our first hostel stay in the country. My neck ached from resting on Austin's shoulder the whole journey, although I'm sure his shoulder would have been in agony just the same. Austin was off the bus first and rushed into the hostel because he needed the toilet desperately. The rest of us grabbed our things and got off. I stretched and stood for a while with my backpack on my shoulders, looking out across the rural span that ran up to the horizon.

Lee had already warned us about landmines even before our planned trip to the Killing Fields near Phnom Penh, but that was because apparently the rural landscape of Cambodia was lined with landmines and we'd stay safe with Lee and the rest of the group.

However, we were staying at our first hostel for one very particular reason. Angkor Wat. An iconic temple with impressive carvings and a huge moat that surrounded the complex. It was pretty spectacular during the day, aside from the sweltering heat, but our plan was to wake up early in the morning and watch the sunrise.

I lugged my bag into the hostel and checked in with the rest of the girls, each of us showing our passports at the request of the hostel.

"Fleur, this is for you." At first, I was thrilled, thinking it was some sort of welcome gift from the hostel. Then I remembered I wasn't staying in a five-star hotel and welcome gifts were not to be expected.

The sweet lady held out a small package wrapped in brown paper. I opened it with the girls and the hostel staff looking over my shoulder.

A flower. Another single flower, but this time a magnificent lily with its stem holding onto another handwritten note. I ignored it for a second, taking in the flower's beauty––mostly white with purple running through the centre of the petals. I took in a deep breath, inhaling its scent, which tickled my nose and forced me to sneeze.

The staff at the hostel thought the gesture was romantic, but I didn't know what to think of it. Receiving one flower at a hostel in one country was one thing, but then having arrived in an entirely different country and to receive another from the same person was bordering on many things––romantic, creepy and weird. Goosebumps rose on my arm despite the dry heat that not even the hostel could shelter us from.

"You've got a stalker. You've got a stalker," Paige teased with the others, willing me to read the note. I was starting to think Paige might be right.

Missing you like a flower misses the sun and rain x

It had to be Connor. Of course he missed me. He and my parents were the only people who had copies of my itinerary and my parents certainly wouldn't have sent me notes like that. But I couldn't help but doubt my gut, just like Andrea's husband made me doubt myself. The gesture, whether I found the act to be romantic or stalker-like, was still undecided, but Connor had never done anything like this before. I'd rarely received flowers from him, let alone to an address that wasn't mine. Although, Connor hadn't messed up this badly before. I could picture him speaking the words written on the note, his beautiful face begging for my forgiveness, but I also didn't know if what I pictured was a compilation of things I wanted to hear.

"A very pretty flower," the Cambodian lady said as she gave us back our passports and we went upstairs to unload our things. Our time set quickly on that day, with an early evening meal and an even earlier bedtime to prepare us for the three in the morning wake up call.

J ust twenty minutes after waking up, we were all on our tuk tuks ready to head to Angkor Wat. My hair looked like birds had nested in it overnight, and my energy levels were as low as they'd ever been without my usual cups of coffee to perk me up in the mornings. I welcomed the slightly cool breeze from the journey as our tuk tuk rushed down roads that were nothing more than dirt tracks with more potholes than level roads.

The tuk tuks dropped us off in the parking lot around a ten minute walk from Angkor Wat, where we had to queue to have our pictures taken for them to be added to our tickets. It was the weirdest thing.

I'd only seen the sunrise a handful of times in my life, but as the sky started to pink along the horizon, my feet moved as fast as they could to beat the crowds of tourists that gathered as I worried we'd all miss the moment I'd dreamed of seeing.

Around five minutes later and holding tightly onto

my torch, I flicked it off as the most beautiful sight graced my eyes.

Angkor Wat and its five towers sat underneath the sky.

We gathered around the moat and I readied my camera to take pictures in order to journal about it later.

The horizon was purple, then a light pink, with the colour coming to life above us and making the sky glow. Until it couldn't contain its beauty anymore. Until the moat mirrored the sunrise perfectly.

"It's so beautiful, isn't it?" I said to Austin who was standing close to me, snapping photos on his phone already attached to a portable charger.

"It really is."

The sky became orange, dark but bright, and then quickly had its colour drained as the sun crept above one of the towers of the temple. The whole thing was an experience I was never going to forget.

I struggled to catch my breath after all I'd seen that morning, seemingly feeling the same way as the person who had been sending me those flowers.

Chapter Fifteen

My legs had never ached as much as they did the following morning after trekking around the beauty that was Angkor Wat. I hopped out of bed with a spring in my step, unaware of the effect that would have on my bones, which clicked and creaked with every movement. I wasn't a morning person, not even as a child, but the constant early mornings we all had to face in order to cram in the itinerary during our trip seemed to be converting me. And I was happy, which also helped––

stress free and not a care in the world. As much as randomly receiving flowers was becoming a little bit of a nuisance, I couldn't help the warmth it filled me with knowing Connor was missing me. It made all the heartache worth it.

The whole group woke up as I was finishing my morning coffee. They all rushed about to pack up their bags, ready for the six hour journey straight to the Killing Fields just outside of Phnom Penh. I sipped the last of my coffee and smirked smugly at Austin, who couldn't find his pants. Walking around the hostel in just his boxer shorts could have been considered offensive, but the people working around us didn't seem to flinch as he rushed past them, hurling abuse at Keira––the only culprit in his eyes and the rightful trouser thief. I held my coffee cup near my mouth and snickered behind it. How could I not feel incredible with those loons around me? With each minute I spent with them, I felt more life being injected into me like a shot of vitamins––vitamins my body had been deficient in for so long.

The coach journey started off at a decent pace, but the closer we got to Phnom Penh, the more tuk tuks weaved around the bus, dodging traffic until we were crawling. I lifted my head to face the aircon and allowed its cool breeze to blast my face for a moment as the sun shone through the window and became unbearable.

"Stop hogging the breeze," Austin said, playfully shoving me closer to the window and then pointing the fan to him.

"Oh no, na-ah. What happened to the chivalrous Austin? The one that goes and gets me drinks from the bar and shares his food?"

"He died in this heat." His face was straight, as serious as I'd ever seen it, until it wasn't anymore. Until laughter took over the both of us and he wrapped his arm around me, squeezing me as tight as he could. I rested my head on his shoulder and waited out the rest of the journey there. Austin was giving off as much heat as the sun but with both of the aircon nozzles having been adjusted and rightfully pointing at me, I was as happy as I was ever going to be on a six hour coach journey.

We walked a short distance up to the genocidal centre at the Killing Fields, with the most luscious green grass growing on the right.

"Guys, look at this," Paige shouted, and we all gathered around her to see a small bone poking out of the ground. And there were more. Different bones were scattered in the patch of grass leading us to a tree, where a skull had been impaled and the bark of the tree had grown around it, almost like it was trying to swallow the devastating history of Cambodia.

I could feel my cheeks shake, my mouth quivering as I tried to hold back all my emotions in front of the others, but it was the sight of Courtney and Keira, the happiest people I'd met, crying that set me off. I wondered if I'd make it to the end of the tour without crying again, but I had no hope.

I placed on the headphones and played the audio tour as I stayed as close as I could to the others. I listened to the tour guide explaining the brutality of nearly a quarter of the population being killed as I walked into the central building to see a cabinet filled with skulls and bones. I felt a lot of things that day—my heart ached for the people of Cambodia and their suffering, but most of all I was angry. Angry that there had been no real justice.

I shuddered as I walked the remainder of the tour, my emotions so high, all I could do was shut down. I was exhausted, even after leaving the Killing Fields. My body had been drained of all its energy, all its happiness, and the spring in my step had disappeared into the abyss. Nothing seemed to pull me from the sadness that had burnt deep into my heart—not the sight of Keira and Courtney cuddling up back on the bus ready to head to our new accommodation and not even Paige being chatted up by a group of young men on some sort of lads' holiday.

"I asked my dog what's two minus two. He said nothing."

Not even Austin and his persistent dad jokes were enough for me to crack a smile. Not a real one, anyway. I rubbed my shoulders as they thanked me for the short break I'd given them while being on the bus and not having to carry my rucksack around.

I then turned away from Austin––away from his smiles and smirks, and just sat, looking out of the window at the world rushing past us.

It was only when everyone started moving off the bus, I snapped back into the moment––away from the poverty and death and back with my friends. They all scurried off the bus quickly with a promise from Lee that we were staying at a hotel that night and not a hostel. The thought of a mattress thicker than a few inches definitely appealed to me, so I gathered my bag up and placed it on my shoulder before being the last person to make my way off the bus.

"Are you okay?" the driver asked as I was about to step off.

"I'm fine, thank you." I gave him a smile, placed my hand in my trouser pocket and pulled out my purse, handing the elderly man some Riel. I didn't need to tip him, but he didn't need to check on me either.

"Akun," he said, placing his hands together to thank me, so I returned his gesture and stepped off the bus in order to catch up with my friends.

Everyone else had already checked in to the hotel, running off to their own bedrooms, with Kiera and Courtney the only ones sharing a room.

"Checking in," I said casually, placing my passport on the counter.

In seconds, my passport was slid back to me along with my room key. My room was on the first floor, and I assumed I was placed in a room close to the others because I could hear Keira screaming at the top of her lungs in excitement.

I entered the room, which was clean and not crammed with bunk beds. Instead, a double bed was placed up against the wall, making it seem like there was more room than there actually was. The walls may have been thin and there weren't any modern commodities like the ones I was used to at home, but I'd have taken a stay there each and every time over a hostel.

I fell back onto the bed in a starfish motion and stretched out as much as I could. My body ached as I sat up with some difficulty and noticed a brown package on the table.

Another flower.

I opened the package like every other time. However, this time I didn't read the note––this time, somehow, opening the package felt different. Was it the pain and suffering I'd seen at the Killing Fields that was still wreaking havoc in my mind and body, or was I fed up with Connor sending flowers? If he really wanted to apologise, he could have got on a plane and come and told me how sorry he was.

I reached into my bag, placed my phone on charge and paced, waiting for it to switch itself back on and have enough power for me to make a call.

The phone rang. I didn't care that Cambodia was seven hours ahead. I didn't care that he had likely done a night shift at the bar last night and was probably still sleeping. I wanted answers. I needed him to answer.

"Fleur, what's up?" His voice cracked as he answered, sounding sleepy.

"What the hell do you think you're doing? Why do you think it's okay to send me flowers to apologise? You made a mistake by leaving. You broke my heart, Connor. You know exactly where I am. You keep sending these flowers, so why not come yourself?" My heart was like a jug and I poured it from full to empty.

"What flowers?" He sounded confused, like he was so tired he didn't fully understand what I'd just said to him.

"I've been getting flowers. I've had three given to me in three different places. I thought it was you, wanting to apologise for breaking up with me over the phone. I thought you'd realised you made a mistake." My hand wrapped around the phone with the wire still plugged in. I couldn't walk and pace like I normally would have. I had to stand there, still, and listen to his words as they ripped my heart into more pieces. I thought it had been broken enough.

"Fleur, I am sorry I broke up with you over the phone. That's something I won't ever forget and I'll live to regret, but I'm not sorry we broke up. That was the right thing, for both of us." His voice was soft, not angry like mine. He was at peace with his decision, something I thought I'd found but I clearly hadn't.

"Right for both of us how?"

"We're both able to live our lives the way we want to. We aren't accountable to each other anymore. I can't hold you back anymore than you can hold me back?"

"Holding you back from what?"

"From finding someone who puts me first."

"Seriously?"

"Fleur, you're angry, and I've been messaging you because I thought we could get through this like adults. I thought we'd be able to be friends..."

I hung up, mid lecture. I wasn't about to deal with his spiel—the speech he'd clearly rehearsed so many times in his head to make him feel better about breaking my heart.

I burst into tears, and within seconds there was knocking at my door. Repetitive knocking.

"Open the door. Let us in." Voices crept through the small gaps left between the door and the frame. "We're not going away until you let us in."

I got up and walked to the door, trying not to fall over as my eyes streamed. My vision may have been blurred, but I couldn't mistake the four figures as anyone else but my friends.

"We heard you having an argument with yourself, so we assumed you were speaking to Connor?" Paige said as each one of them stepped in and sat on my bed. "What's happened?"

"I got another flower so I called him to tell him that I'd appreciate an apology in person instead of the flowers. Turns out it wasn't him and he isn't sorry at all. I knew I was angry at him and I would have found it very hard to forgive him, but the truth is, I know I would have jumped at the chance of us being back together. I'm such an idiot."

"You needed this to happen. You needed closure, girl. Now you've got it. Now you can move on." Keira got up from the bed and wrapped her arms around me, followed by the rest of the gang. I smiled through my sadness and looked over at the flower sitting on the table.

I loosened my hug and made my way over to the flower. I picked up the daisy by its stem and looked at the colours that seemed to brighten up the room. I held it close to my heart and shut my eyes.

If Connor wasn't sending these flowers, who was?

I picked up the note. The writing held no resemblance to the first or second flowers I'd received. They had all been written by different people.

"This isn't some sort of practical joke between you all, is it?"

"What? Are you serious?" Paige said, her eyebrows pointed at the accusation.

"Yes. Each note is written by someone different."

"It isn't me," Kiera quickly said, defending her pride.

"So it's not a joke? You're not all winding me up because I'm the eldest here?"

"It's definitely not a joke, I promise," Austin said with sincerity lining his words.

"Okay," I said as he placed his arm on me. I looked back at the note, this time not looking at the calligraphy, and read it out loud.

Don't let anyone or anything stop you from smiling x

Chapter Sixteen

I started the following day like any other. Coffee. Gallons of coffee, and then responded to messages received from Janine and Andrea. Texts like *How are the travels going, abandoner?* and *When are you coming home?* I told them about my penis tattoo, which they both found hilarious. Aside from the itchiness, I was getting used to it and it brought a pretty big smile to my face each time I caught a glimpse of it.

We had pretty much a whole day free before we

were due to leave Cambodia and get an overnight bus to Vietnam. As a group, we decided to explore Phnom Penh in all its glory, and even Lee decided to join us despite it being one of our free days to do what we liked. We strolled the paths of the Mekong River and then tried plenty of food. My stomach may have been fit to explode but my taste buds craved more delicious food. Then we drank. And I drank a little more than everyone else.

"We're going to be late. Come on," Lee yelled from a good few metres away, as I swayed in and out of the crowds and forced Austin to do the same as he clung to me. If anything, the amount of booze I'd drunk was going to help me sleep on the bus.

"We will make it. We've got this," Austin said, practically holding me up straight. He also had my bag on his back, because I was in no state to carry it for myself.

"Yeah, take a chill pill," I slurred, and then burst into fits of laughter. I found myself hilarious.

The serious thing was, this bus wasn't organised for the tour. It was an overnight bus that anyone could use and it wasn't going to wait for anyone.

"Wait," Lee billowed out to the bus with its doors still open. He ran ahead of us even further to get on.

"Is Lee leaving us? Pfft. Some tour guide."

"No, he's not. You're drunk and he's making the bus wait for us."

"Oh. Wooo! Go, Lee!" I cheered him on like an olympian running the hundred metres.

I hopped onto the bus, curtsied to the driver and stumbled down the aisle to find an empty seat.

I didn't remember much more of that night, but my wonderful friends continued to remind me for the rest of the trip that I managed to throw up a lot. And that I owed Paige a new bag. It would have been cheaper to just pay the driver a cleaning fee.

Ho Chi Minh City. The death city as I nicknamed it. The only way to cross the road was through gritted teeth, taking each step without looking at the cars and motorcycles that weaved in between them because if I were to look, I would have hesitated and probably would have died. I didn't fit in there. You could spot locals a mile off who would just casually stroll across the road without flinching, despite the traffic rushing past them. The city was the king of overpopulation and I didn't like it. All the traffic had me feeling like I couldn't breathe as I stood at the edge of the roadside looking out to seven lanes each way. I would have had better luck crossing the M1 in London.

I had nowhere to go to escape the mayhem of the city, so that evening I decided to book a flight a day earlier than everyone else on the tour. Instead of staying in Ho Chi Minh City for another day, I could be in Hoi An by myself. The peace and quiet wouldn't do me any harm either.

"Are you seriously leaving us?"

"It will do me good. I need time to think. Besides, it's only for a day then I'll be seeing you there. I'll remember to take note of all the best places to eat." I sat in the taxi with the windows down.

"Traitor!" Paige yelled.

"Miss you too!" I smiled and waved then wound the window back up, allowing the cool aircon to fill the car on the way to the airport.

I ended up spending more time in the airports than I did on that flight, but Hoi An was totally worth it. The houses were painted different shades of yellow and orange, and their colours reflected beautifully in the river as the sun set. I checked into a hostel for the one night before the rest of the group were due to join me.

Hoi An was a smaller place, quieter, and it felt like The Netherlands of Vietnam. I felt like I could breathe. The ground was wet from rain and the scent it left behind was fresh and clean.

I filled my lungs with the fresh air as I stepped out of the hostel the next morning and sat in a small coffee shop, positioning myself so I looked directly out to the river. I watched the multicoloured lanterns that were hung from the trees and buildings as they swayed in the light, pleasant breeze that only seemed to exist in the early or late hours of the day. I watched locals walk past with their shopping––they weren't in a rush like in the big city. The streets were vacant of tourists and I didn't know if it was too early for them or if I'd found an idyllic little corner of Vietnam that I could soak up all to myself.

I pulled out my travel journal, along with polaroid pictures I'd captured, and began to document my travels so far. I'd barely had a chance to think about my journal as we'd been so busy, but I made time and I was so glad of it. I must have just about finished The Netherlands when an elderly lady sat on the same table as me. I thought it was a little weird as there were plenty of free tables in the cafe, but I smiled and then continued to glue pictures and write about my travels.

"Bạn trông có vẻ buồn, nhưng bạn không cô đơn."

"I'm sorry, I don't speak Vietnamese."

She gave me a small smile, and placed her hand on mine. Her touch was gentle, consoling me. I placed my hand on hers and squeezed it a little.

I continued to journal as she watched my every

move. I pulled a picture of the tulip fields at my child-hood house from the pile. It had been taken just a few minutes before Connor had broken my heart. I wanted to tear the picture up and erase the memory of it from my mind, but I had to look on the bright side. I was halfway around the globe, living out my dream of trav-elling and had someone sending me flowers. It was also an hour or so after that memory when I'd met Levi, and I hadn't really thought about him since leaving The Netherlands. It was only as I saw his number written at the back of my journal I remembered how he'd made me feel––world's apart from Connor. He'd noticed me in an entirely different way. He'd under-stood me.

Just came across your number in the back of my travel diary while journaling. I hope you're doing okay?

I pressed send after putting a kiss at the end of the message and deleting it many times over. I wondered if he had thought about me. I even wondered if it was him sending the flowers. He had been in my journal to write his number down so he could have known my itinerary. I shook off the thought and decided that the person would show up sooner or later. I was going to enjoy the admiration for a little while longer, at least. I was finally at peace with receiving the flowers and allowed myself to enjoy the tranquillity of Hoi An until I couldn't anymore.

"Oh heyyyyyy!" The silence that surrounded me had been obliterated but I had missed them. It had been around twenty-four hours since I'd last seen them—not long in the grand scheme of things but when you were alone in a foreign country where not many people spoke your language, it felt like a long time.

"I've missed you guys," I said, each one giving me a hug. Paige's hug was drawn out, squeezing me as tight as she could. Courtney's was brief, yet a kiss on my cheek from her made me feel so warm. Keira's hug was playful and ended with us shimmying our boobs together, which from the moment I'd met her in that backpackers' bar was something I'd never thought I'd do, but she made me feel so alive. Austin wrapped his arms around me, his strong grip gently binding me to him.

"Missed you more," he said as his hand repositioned some of my hair. "You smell nice. Is that a new perfume?"

"Of course it is. I couldn't resist the urge to shop. I've actually been able to look without you guys causing havoc. You're all bulls in China shops."

"Excuse me, little miss perfect, but I seem to remember you being very drunk less than forty-eight hours ago. I'm sure there must be a warrant out for your arrest. P.S. you still owe me a new bag." Paige smirked at me.

"Ah, well that's where this will help." I pulled out a brand new leather handbag, with an intricate cross stitch design. It was perfect for Paige and big enough for the thousands of items she'd stored in her old bag.

"Oh my gosh, that's so gorgeous. Eeek, thank you!" Paige gave me another hug before continuing to tease me. "I might get you drunk more often if it means I get brand new bags like this one. Speaking of drunk... who fancies a drink before we watch the lanterns?"

"Sign me up." It was a no brainer, really.

After a few drinks in a bar close to the river, the banks and sidewalks started to become crowded. A mixture of locals and tourists got ready to see a moment so magical it seemed to belong in a Disney movie. That didn't stop us from getting a prime position, with the river on one side and a cocktail bar on the other.

The sun lay to rest for another day as it drifted below the horizon, making room for the stars in the night sky. The lanterns that hung above us were switched on, illuminating a quivering path across the river. I could hear music underneath the crowds talking and cheering, and Kiera tapped along to the beat on her knees.

"Oh my God, look," Paige yelled, jumping up from a cross-legged position in excitement, wanting to get a better look. Warmly coloured lanterns floated along the river, with the current carrying them downstream. Each one had different patterns and flickered uniquely as it fought to stay lit and survive its journey down the river.

"They are so beautiful," Austin began as I fought back tears. A rush of overwhelming emotion ran through me as I took in a sight I'd longed to see. It was as beautiful as I'd imagined. I was in love with Hoi An and everything it had to offer, just like I'd always known I would be, but I never imagined how much joy I'd get from sharing the moment with my favourite people in the world. "It almost reminds me of that Disney movie, Tangled."

"Yes!"

"It does!"

The rest of them agreed but I had no idea what they were on about. I didn't have time for movies, let alone movies made for children. "What do you mean? I've not seen it."

"You've not seen Tangled?" Keira and Courtney screeched in unison, and seemed offended, like I'd committed a hate crime.

"It was a take on the story of Rapunzel, where she is born into royalty and kidnapped as a young child. Each year on the princess' birthday, the whole kingdom lights lanterns that float in the sky and along the river to remember her."

"Aww that sounds lovely. I want to watch it."

I sat cuddling against Austin and Paige as the final few lanterns sailed past us, and then we watched the glow disappear from the sky above.

"Oh no, I forgot to take pictures." I scrambled to take my camera out of my bag, panic driven and wanting to salvage one of the most magical moments of my travels so far. It was up there, along with The Netherlands, meeting Levi and being with this crazy bunch.

"That's okay, don't worry. You are never going to forget this night. I know I won't." Austin shuffled closer and pulled me into him with his arm. We must have been in the same spot for a few more hours until we went to our hostel, watching stars fill in spaces in the black sky as the bars closed one by one, each turning off their lanterns.

The next morning, I woke a little later than everyone else, with all the early starts catching up on me. I made my way downstairs and sat on one of the very few chairs in the hostel reception after scouring the local streets to find a decent coffee.

"Hey, you!" Austin bounced in. I'd never seen him so happy in the mornings. It could have been because of the beauty last night, or the fact that the girls weren't pranking him like they normally would have been.

I smiled at him from behind my coffee, still a little too early to communicate even to the best of people.

"I meant to ask you. Have you received a flower while you've been here? You hadn't said?"

"No," I croaked. "No flower."

"Oh, well, maybe these will make up for not receiving one."

Austin handed over a handful of postcards, each one displaying an image of the lanterns and each one different from the next.

"Oh my, these are gorgeous. There are so many of them."

"Twenty-seven," he said, pleased with himself. "I thought at least one of them would be perfect for you to journal."

I pushed myself off the seat and placed the post-cards in my place. My hands met with Austin's face, and with my touch, his eyes closed.

"You're incredible." I kissed him on his cheek and pulled myself as close to him as I could. "We best head to the airport. If Lee was mad about us nearly missing a bus, can you imagine his face if we were to miss a plane?" I laughed.

Travelling was going just as I'd planned, my dreams becoming a real, vivid reality. I'd started to rely on the friends I'd made during my trip for love, laughter and everything in between, something I'd never thought I would. I had always been a bit of a lone-wolf, but I'd realised how much my life had improved with them in it. With Paige, Keira and Courtney, my crazy gals, and Austin, my best friend, life couldn't have been any better.

Chapter Seventeen

"How does it look?" Paige asked as she bobbed above the calm waves that lapped around her. The midday heat only seemed bearable after taking a dip in the blue waters of Halong Bay.

Paige wanted me to film a TikTok video of them all jumping off the boat and into the sea, all doing different superhero poses. I'd tried countless times to get it right, but each of them messed up at least once.

Until we got the perfect take. Until I forgot to press record.

They're going to kill me.

"It didn't record. I don't know why," I said through gritted teeth.

"No, Fleur!" Paige looked as if she was about to have an emotional breakdown. "Right, everyone out. Let's do it again," she commanded.

"Really? Can we not be happy with the one where Austin forgot what pose he was doing? We can just crop him out if not," Keira jested and in return, Austin launched a surge of water at her with all the force of his biceps.

"No. We're going to do this properly, for me. Fleur has her travel journal where she can keep memories, Austin doesn't care about keeping memories and you two have your lovey-dovey girlfriends travelling Instagram account. Absolutely sickening by the way. We're doing this for me and my TikTok." Paige climbed up the ladder and got back into position, occasionally turning to the others to encourage them to get back on the boat quicker.

Once they were ready, I gave Paige the nod, making sure to press the record button, and watched each of them act like a superhero of their choice. Keira and

Courtney were Mystique and Catwoman, because apparently if we lived in a parallel universe, they'd have been lesbian lovers. Austin acted out being Captain America because he dreamt of one day having arms like Chris Evans. Paige was Scarlet Witch, because she was the most powerful, and none of us were about to argue and face her wrath. I watched and recorded on the sidelines, like their mother. They said I would have been Wonder Woman: caring, opinionated, competitive and protects the innocent, and though I didn't know much about Wonder Woman, I had to agree.

And modest, too.

The video looked awesome in reverse, watching each of my friends emerge from the water and land on the boat as if by magic.

"Do me, do me!" I yelled, ready to jump into the water after waving my arms and standing with my hands on my hips in a way that seemed to resemble Wonder Woman.

I jumped into the water, allowing the pressure underneath to turn my world silent for a few seconds. I opened my eyes as they adjusted to the salt water, looked at the hull of the boat, and watched fish swimming around me as if they had no care in the world. I peered my head out of the water, my ears still muffled and my eyes glazed over from the water as I took in the view. The blue of the water spanned as far as the eye could see, and huge rocks with greenery grew from underneath. I could have sworn I was in Avatar and not Vietnam. I almost didn't want to head back to the hostel and leave Vietnam for good. I almost decided not to leave.

"Fleur, you have another package from your secret lover." I was barely through the hostel door before Austin yelled from the front desk. It was like he'd run in before me to find out. They were more excited than I was. They all gathered around, waiting for me to tear the packaging open to reveal another flower. It was single stem with five flowering shoots of Lavender sat proudly upon it––it was as if an artist had intricately painted the flowers with a deep purple wine. The flowers were pretty enough to take my breath away.

Of all these flowers I've sent to you, you're still the most beautiful of them all x

I let out a sigh and looked away from the flower to see my four favourite people all looking, blinking and waiting for my reaction. Didn't my sigh tell them what they wanted to know?

"Well?"

I loved the flowers, I couldn't deny it, but I was

getting bored with not knowing who the mystery man was. I was fed up with Levi remaining silent, even if he wasn't the one sending them. Why had he not already messaged back? Why would he send me flowers and not own up to it?

I had to pull myself out of the negativity otherwise I would have thrown the flower at the wall. Not that it would have done any good.

It was romantic. This is a romantic gesture.

I told myself––it had to be part of something bigger. I just had to wait and be patient––something I knew I wasn't very good at.

"It's nice, isn't it? And the note is lovely, too," I said and then asked for a cup to place the flowers in.

"I wish you'd send me flowers and messages like this," Keira said to Courtney, her face joking but her tone serious.

"I don't need to. You know how much I love you. Fleur's secret admirer clearly doesn't know if she loves them or not."

Keira let out an uncertain noise and then carried on about her business, checking in with the rest of us.

We headed to our room to have a short nap before making our way to Hanoi, Vietnam's capital, famous for its beauty, temples and food. I was a little concerned about going to another big city in Vietnam, especially as I thought back to how much I didn't like Ho Chi Minh City. If it had been any other day, any other trip, I probably would have skipped it and done my own thing. However, I had a reason to be there. That reason was the hostel name that sat in my journal and the possibility of receiving another flower, another note and another piece of the puzzle.

I lay in bed, trying to sleep in a heat that the aircon didn't seem to rectify, and all I could hear was whispering. Angry loud whispering coming from Keira and Courtney as they lay on the same single bed.

"I do love you. Do I not show it enough?"

"Yes, you do. It would just be nice to get nice gifts and messages."

More inaudible whispers filled the room before Courtney stormed out, leaving Keira on the bed, her sniffles becoming uncontrollable sobs. I twisted myself and got out of bed, took her hand and pulled her out of the room. She didn't resist. I could tell she wanted to talk. She was that type of person––open and honest about everything, including her feelings.

"What's wrong?"

"I think I've started some big problem with Court. She thinks I'm unhappy. She thinks she isn't good enough, yet I'm the one that isn't good enough for her.

I shouldn't have said anything," Kiera said, shoving her arms by her side.

"Firstly, you two are meant for each other. I can't think of another couple on this planet that are more meant for each other. Even more so than my own parents." She shrugged my first comment off as if it were untrue. "Secondly, you wouldn't be Keira if you didn't tell her how you feel, and clearly it has been bothering you. You guys will pull through this and it will be good for you both."

"I hope you're right. I'd hate to have booked this trip thinking we can relive the magic and end up going home broken."

"You're going to go home together, happier than you have ever been before. Let's get some rest and let Courtney cool off." We walked back into the room where Austin and Paige were both sleeping and both oblivious to what had happened. If only it was ten years ago and I was able to sleep on demand.

"Where is she?" Lee said, pacing up and down the bus as we all waited––all glaring out of the bus windows, our eyes picking up any movements outside.

"She'll be here," I said. She had to be, especially after what I'd promised Keira. It had been nearly four hours and she'd still not returned. I even had to grab her bags and pack up everything she'd been using because she was cutting it close.

Lee spoke to the driver in a language I couldn't decipher before pacing back up to the back of the bus where we were sitting.

"The driver will have to leave soon. He can't wait all night."

"He can, and he will. We all will if it comes to that." I spoke with a stern professional voice I'd not used since being in a court, hoping it still had the sway it had back home, but before Lee could do anything, the engine rumbled and the doors shut.

"I'm getting off the bus. I'm not leaving without her." Keira grabbed her bag and ran to the front of the bus in a panic, but just as the driver was about to open the door to allow her to leave, there she was.

Courtney was kneeling on the floor holding a small box. She looked at Keira with tears in her eyes that must have been burning her face in the heat. We all looked out with our faces pressed against the windows to not miss a second of the moment.

The driver opened the door and Courtney started speaking. We couldn't hear properly, but you could see the love that radiated off them both, and that was all I needed.

"Talk louder, we can't hear you!" Austin yelled

from the bus, immediately making everyone on the bus laugh, and it cracked up the happy couple, too.

"Fine!" Courtney shouted from her knelt down position. "Keira, each day you fill me with so much joy. You're the happiest person I know. Your infectious laughter and smile, your sense of humour and your kindness are things I fell in love with while we were travelling the first time, and this trip has allowed me to fall in love with them all over again. I'd be honoured if you'd become my wife. Will you?"

"Do you even need to ask? I would have said yes the minute I met you. I love you so much." Keira stepped off the bus and they both met in a loving embrace. We all ran down the bus cheering, and even the strangers who were to join us on the bus journey ahead started to applaud them.

"I love you more," Courtney said to Keira and we huddled around them, practically smothering each other to the point where we all had sweat dripping from our foreheads once we'd finished.

"I hate to break this up, but the driver is ready to hit the accelerator, and we have a new city to get to."

At Lee's orders, we jumped back on the bus, each of us apologising to the driver in our own way and sat ready to depart to Hanoi––excited to explore a new city with the soon to be Mrs and Mrs.

"I hope that one day I'm as happy as them," Austin said, peering through the gap in the seats from in front.

"Me too."

Around three hours later, we arrived in Hanoi just as the sky was darkening and the cityscape lit up like stars in the night. Our hostel was opposite the Hoan Kiem Lake and we were only staying in the beautiful Hanoi for one night, so we thought we'd make the most of it.

We purchased some alcohol and sat looking out across the lake. The still water could have been mistaken for ice if it hadn't been so warm.

"I wonder what that temple is for? Nobody can even get to it," Paige said, observing the temple that stood magnificently, isolated by the water.

"Yeah, if only boats existed." Keira sniggered under her breath, but loud enough for Paige to glare at her.

"It's called the Turtle Tower," Austin said as he scrolled through the internet on his phone. "Apparently, some huge, magical turtle emerged and took a sword from a warrior that helped free Vietnam from Chinese oppression."

"Are you high?" Paige laughed and took a large gulp of her drink.

"No, why? That's what it says here."

I held my plastic cup in the air and waited for everyone else to follow.

"Well, here's to being the best of friends, this gorgeous lake, the happy soon-to-be-wed couple and magic turtles and shit." Our glasses met with a clink and our laughter lasted long into the night, until our stomachs hurt and we couldn't laugh anymore.

Chapter Eighteen

The following morning I woke with a slightly sore head, overlooked by Austin in the bed next to me.

"Morning, sleepyhead," he said. His head was perched on his pillow and his body cocooned in a beige blanket.

"Morning," I croaked back. "What time is it?"

"About nine-ish. We should probably think about getting up. The others have been up for an hour or so.

They have already left to explore, but before they went they told me to tell you that there is another package for you downstairs at the desk."

Before he could finish speaking, I jumped out of bed wearing the skimpiest of pyjamas in order to stay cool but still conceal my modesty, and started to gather my things ready to go downstairs. Austin looked as though he'd already been up and about, dressed in his normal casual wear. He followed me downstairs like a lost puppy; he had for most of the trip. I assumed it was because we were both from the UK so had something in common.

I stepped up to the desk and asked for my parcel, still wearing what I'd slept in. The hostel had probably seen a lot worse.

I teared open the white paper that covered the box, which held the inevitable flower. I was excited to see its beauty, no matter what kind it was. A gorgeous lotus flower, the national flower of Vietnam, sat in a beautiful casing and had a handwritten note.

The perfect flower to sum up last night together x

My breath got caught in my throat as I looked to Austin with a smile, beaming from ear to ear.

"Have you been sending me these flowers?" I asked as I ran my finger across one of the pink lotus petals.

He grabbed hold of my free hand and looked deep into my eyes––a meaningful gaze like the ones you'd see in a movie as characters are about to kiss. A look that said *I've been here the whole time.*

"I have. Do you like it?"

I tried to swallow the lump that had formed in my throat. "It's beautiful."

I struggled to find the words to say, caught off guard and vulnerable like a solicitor defending a client with no case.

"I asked you all if you were sending me these flowers. You said no."

"No, Fleur. I said it wasn't a practical joke. The minute we sat in the Mad Monkey Bar underneath our hostel and I started talking to you, I knew exactly how I felt about you. I knew I wanted what Keira and Courtney have, but with you." He smiled, still holding onto my hand, and then pulled me into his chest and held onto me like he didn't ever want to let go. His hand ran through my hair and he kissed my forehead.

How had I not seen him? How had I not known about his feelings?

As I started to relive the memories I'd made with

Austin, I realised I'd mistaken his love for friendship and kindness. He'd purchased twenty-seven postcards for me because I'd forgotten to take pictures of the floating lanterns; he'd made sure I was safe when I'd had far too much to drink and even tried to cheer me up after our visit to the Killing Fields.

"You are happy it's me and not Connor, right?" He looked concerned.

If he'd asked me that a couple of weeks earlier, I would have been lying if I'd said I was. I was at peace that Connor and I were not getting back together. Could I deny that I wanted it to be someone else? Someone I'd struggled to stop thinking about since I'd stopped hanging onto the thought of Connor and I being a couple again. Levi had comforted me the day my whole life had fallen apart, everything I'd ever known, and I'd set my heart on him fixing me piece by piece. I'd thought it was him sending the flowers.

"I'm happy it's you and not Connor," I said, batting away my true feelings. Austin was a nice guy, someone I considered my best friend and someone I pictured seeing even after travelling and being back at home. I hadn't pictured the possibility of us going back to the UK as something other than friends, but that didn't mean it couldn't happen.

"Do the girls know you've been sending the flowers all this time?"

"Absolutely not. They wouldn't have been able to keep it a secret."

"You have a point to be fair." I laughed. "I wonder what they will say. You know they were as invested in the flowers as I was. Shall we tell them today?"

"We could, although wouldn't it be fun to wait? To keep us secret? I think we should wait. I don't want to steal the newly engaged thunder. Besides, is there even anything to tell yet? At the moment I'm just a guy that's been sending a gorgeous woman some flowers. I don't even know if you like me." His eyes widened like a puppy, watching, waiting for an answer. Waiting to hear the words he desperately wanted to hear.

"You're right. Let's wait. Let's get to know each other a bit more without the girls screaming and getting excited," I said, ignoring his last statement, because I liked him, loved him even, but all I felt for him was friendship and nothing more.

Once we were ready, Austin and I walked the streets of Hanoi and took in its beauty. Buildings towered above us, some seeming ancient and some contemporary, and yet somehow the combination worked.

Occasionally, Austin would wrap a few of his

fingers around mine, subtly trying to hold my hand without being noticed by the girls. I wanted there to be electricity, a buzz running through that connected us on another level. Yet, each time I checked my phone as we strolled through the city and checked my messages to see Levi's name along with no reply, my sadness seemed to dampen anything that Austin and I could have.

I needed to forget about Levi and focus on Austin, so I nipped to the toilet while he ordered us drinks in a cafe on Train Street to text him again.

I've been thinking about you, about us, and I think I read the situation wrong––got us wrong. I'm sorry.

I sat down at the table Austin had picked out for us at the front of the cafe, looking out over the crowded street with a rail track running down the middle of it.

"What have you ordered?" I said, just as a waiter brought over a bottle of Champagne in a bucket of ice. "You ordered Champagne? Why?" I asked once the bottle was placed down and the waiter disappeared.

"I want to make up for the past few weeks we've spent together. I want to show you how I'd treat you if we were in a relationship." His words made me feel fuzzy and warm, and the bubbles from the Champagne tickled my nose as I took my first sip.

"There's nothing wrong with the time we've spent together. You've been an incredible friend and you've helped me become the Fleur I was destined to be. You all have." I spoke from the heart, something I'd always done as a solicitor.

He was my friend, and I didn't know if I could see him as anything other than a younger brother. Every single one of my friends had taught me something, and Austin had taught me about friendship.

"So, let's toast." He raised his glass and I raised mine, just as the street was no longer crowded and the ground started to rumble. "Here's to being amazing friends, and even better lovers."

Fuck.

A train ran down the street, its carriages as busy as the street once had been, with people hanging out of the doors. It bought me some time, but not enough to think of something better to say. Something that would tell him I didn't want to rush into something too quick. Something to say that no matter what happened, I wanted us to stay friends. Instead of saying all those reasonable things, I said something ridiculous.

"To us."

Well done, Fleur. Well done.

As the street filled with crowds once more, I pulled out my phone and messaged Paige to ask where they were. They were only a few streets away and met us in the cafe on Train Street before we could hide any and all evidence of the bottle of Champagne.

"Ooooh, what are you guys celebrating?" Keira said, immediately grabbing my glass and finishing the remnants. "I owe you one."

"We're not celebrating. Fleur said she was missing her home comforts and apparently she drinks Champagne regularly," he said quickly, after thinking of a reason why we'd be drinking bubbles together. "She's a rich bitch," he whispered, and forced a laugh out of everyone.

His reason could have been better.

"Yep. I used to drink Champagne every night in a bubble bath to relax after a hard day of work. That reminds me, I bought this bottle, so it's your round next, isn't it?" I directed my question to Austin and smirked slightly as everyone else pulled a chair around our table.

"Well played. I think I may have met my match with you." He walked back to the bar and I tipped the last of the Champagne into my glass, fighting off Keira at the same time. I may not have known what I wanted, but this girl was not about to pass up a free round of drinks.

"So, now you don't have a job, how are you going to afford Champagne to drink in the bath when you get back home?" Paige asked, clearly not having detected the sarcasm my tongue was laced with when I said it.

"I assume I'll just find a job at a new firm. I've not given it much thought. If I'm honest, I just want to enjoy my travels stress free."

"Oh, I thought you hated it, though? I thought you didn't like the way the men treated you? What happens if you go and work for someone else and it happens again?" she asked, expecting answers to all of her questions. Answers I couldn't give. Not yet, anyhow.

"I'm not sure what my career will look like, but I am sure that my future bosses won't be like Walter. I won't be going back home for months yet, and I know when I do, I'll be a completely different person. The type of woman who doesn't care what men think, the type to grab a man by his balls to make sure I get exactly what I want. The type of woman I used to be before I met Connor and before loving someone became so important."

"I think you're closer to being her again than you think," Courtney said with a smile and then quickly snatched my Champagne flute from the table, taking a sip.

Maybe she was right.

Chapter Nineteen

Of all the travelling we'd done, the sleeper bus from Vietnam to Laos had to be some of the worst and best.

Hour one had all of us playing card games from our seats, sat cross legged in order to create room for our complete sets.

"Do you have any jacks?" Austin turned to ask me, his eyes pleading for me to have his card.

"Go fish." I gave him a smug look.

If our journey had carried on that way, the time spent on the bus wouldn't have seemed so bad.

By hour six, we were all getting sleepy and restless, so we decided to try to sleep to kill some time.

Only seventeen more hours to go.

Sleeping was a great plan—that was until the driver woke us up as the bus came to a stop in what seemed to be the middle of nowhere. The aircon had stopped blowing out the cool refreshing air and the bus became hot and sweaty in minutes.

"Everybody off the bus," Lee said specifically to our group after the driver's instruction.

But why? I could still be sleeping right now. The bus isn't going to explode.

Oh, how wrong I was.

I stood metres away from a bus that blazed at the side of the road as we waited for a replacement to come and pick us up. We didn't know if it would be minutes or hours, but luckily I had grabbed my travel journal and bag before the driver started his pathetic attempt at dousing the fire. We were all okay, sleepy, but safe.

Sleepy Fleur didn't cope well with waiting–– sleepy Fleur was not good at anything aside from drinking coffee.

We arrived by hour thirty. It took six damn hours for a replacement bus to come to take us to our destination. As we stepped off the bus in Vientiane, the capital of Laos, we all exhaled a sigh of relief.

We only had around a week left together, and I wasn't ready to say goodbye to them all, so I promised myself I would make the most of the next week, no matter what.

I checked into our final real hotel of the trip, excited to have a little luxury and drink Champagne in the bath, obviously. There was no flower waiting for me at the desk. I guessed there didn't have to be now that Austin had revealed himself as my mysterious stalker.

I had only just been getting used to receiving flowers and was finally excited about them––and then they were gone.

The following morning, we went to Pha That Luang, a magnificent golden Buddhist temple that stood shadowing the city. It shone bright in the early morning sun. We all stood around it, still a little sleepy, and listened to Lee tell us the temple's history.

Standing there, there was silence as we looked up at its beauty. Until there wasn't quiet anymore.

There was shouting. Angry shouting. From Laos officials.

To make it worse, they were shouting at us.

I had no idea why they were angry. I couldn't

understand them. I quickly looked around to make sure I wasn't standing on some sacred piece of land or artefact. I was safe.

"So, we need to run," Lee said, his feet beginning to move slowly, waiting for ours to follow.

"What, why?" I questioned. I couldn't run from the police. I was a solicitor. I respected the law.

"No time. Run or you'll be arrested."

With that remark, my feet began to move as fast as they could. Sweat dripped from my forehead as I tried to keep up with Austin, feeling as though I was running the London Marathon in excruciating heat.

One by one, we all arrived back at the hotel, each one of us more confused than the other until Lee appeared.

"What the hell was that about?" I panted through each word.

"We were supposed to have a Laotian guide for the tour because it's against the law for me to show you all around. Our tour guide dropped out and well, I didn't think we were going to get caught," Lee said, also breathless.

"So why did we have to run? You're the tour guide. Surely you'd just get in trouble?" I said like the experienced solicitor I was, listening and asking more questions to get all the information I needed. Everyone waited for Lee to answer.

"To be fair, you have a point. I don't know what would have happened. Mostly, I was afraid you'd give them my details."

Everyone sighed at his honesty. That was the first time I'd ever been in trouble. I'd always run towards the law, never against it. I couldn't deny how exhilarating it was––I almost wanted to do it again, without the running.

The next two days found us in many different areas of Laos.

In Luang Prabang, there was no flower waiting for me. However, we got up at the crack of dawn and watched the silent and sacred ceremony where around two hundred monks lined the streets between five and six in the morning. As we made our way to where the monks would be, a car stopped to allow us to cross the road. In some of the other places we'd been, crossing a road could have been considered a dangerous sport, but not there.

We observed from afar, watching them accepting food and personal care items from locals and tourists to provide their sustenance for the day. They were wearing saffron coloured robes and nothing more. No shoes. I couldn't imagine walking around barefoot in the streets, especially later in the day where the sun's heat would turn the pavement into hot coals.

We then stayed near Kuang Si Falls, and there was no flower waiting for me. However, I was able to swim in the bluest of water, and have my picture taken. A picture that was Instagram worthy and of course Paige was the judge of that. The water flowed from the top of a steep hill and the falls created shallow pools that glistened, with rays of light bouncing off effortlessly. It was just as perfect as the pictures I'd seen, and I made sure to snap some photos ready to journal them.

I swam under the falls into a small, eroded cave, holding my breath as the water battered me from above, and Austin followed me.

"This place is magical," I said, wiping water from my brows as I bobbed up and down above the small waves created by the falls.

"It really is." Austin swam towards me, closing the space that once separated us. He looked behind us to see nothing but water, and then kissed me. It was a good kiss––soft, but firm. His hands held onto me like he never wanted to let go.

"You're so beautiful," he said, as he pulled away from my lips, and at the sound of someone else swimming underneath the falls, we added further space between us and tried not to make eye contact. My heart thumped as fast as it could as I took in my surroundings. Adrenaline pumped through my body as the water crashed against my hand as it fell so beautifully. Austin's kiss was sweet and his words were sweeter, but nothing could compare to feeling as though I was a princess living a real life fairy tale––a fairy tale I wanted to continue to live. I was in no position to accept my happily ever after.

Our final place in Laos was Vang Vieng, and there was no flower waiting for me. However, we went tubing along the river. We all sat in a rubber ring, using our hands to push ourselves along in the murky water. Occasionally, different bars that lined the river would throw in some ropes so we could pull ourselves up the bank of the river and out of the water. Each one had a different vibe, some with music blasting from the speakers, the beat enticing us to come ashore, and others more chilled.

"Yes, Keira!" I yelled as a ping pong ball landed in the opponent's final cup. The lads' faces were priceless having been beaten by a group of girls, and Austin, of course. After beating them at beer pong, they followed us down the river and we played a multitude of other games in a variety of bars in our drunken state. It was nice to let my hair down, something I'd done a lot of during my time travelling and not a lot of beforehand.

"Where's Paige?" I asked the rest of the gang as we sat around a wooden table. Austin was practically drooling, his mouth wide open, and pointed behind me. Paige was being pressed up against a wall by one of the lads. They couldn't have been closer to each other as his lips wrapped around hers and his hands wandered all over her perfect body. For a second, I pictured Levi and how he'd made me feel before the guilt quickly pulled me out of my daydream.

Damn, he's hot.

I gawped at him unnecessarily, just as Austin had done to Paige. The guy was likely nearly half my age, but that didn't matter. A woman could look.

And then it hit me like the bus nearly had done in Vietnam.

Austin had been very kindly sending me those flowers, and he wasn't bad looking. In fact, he was pretty hot and kind, but he was also a bit of a douche, and immature. I didn't see him in the same way that I had with Connor or Levi, because they were men and not a young lad trying to find his footing in the world. Austin was a friend, and I doubted I'd ever see him as more than that.

As Austin looked at Paige, I even started to wonder if I was what he truly wanted. Was he just lonely? Did he think I was an easy catch? Did he think I'd just be another notch on his bedpost? Probably. Or was drooling over Paige an act he was putting on to try to convince Keria and Courtney that nothing was going on between us?

No matter what the case was, I knew I had a decision to make, and I had to make it before leaving South East Asia for good. And there was only one destination left on our itinerary before heading back to Bangkok.

I woke up to noises—noises that sounded like someone was in pain but they also could have been mistaken for pleasure. I rubbed my eyes as they adjusted to the dim lighting of the hostel and looked to Austin who was rolling around on his bed, holding on to his stomach.

"What's up?" I whispered, trying not to wake the others. If they were going to wake up, it wouldn't have been my whispers that woke them, but the moans and groans of Austin.

"My stomach kills. I keep being sick," he whined in between rough noises.

"Do you have food poisoning?" I asked, getting out of bed unwillingly. The amount of travel we'd done towards the end of the trip had started to catch up on me. I wasn't looking forward to saying my good-byes, but I couldn't wait to spend a week back in Bangkok where I'd be able to do nothing more than lounge around a hotel and book my next destinations. And drink Champagne in the bath, of course.

"That would explain the sickness," he muttered, still as sarcastic as ever, even in his state.

I dodged his vomit as I tiptoed to his bed, and forced him to move from his statuesque position as he hunched himself over the bed. I eventually got him to the toilet, shutting the door behind him as he launched himself to the basin, clinging on to the seat. I ran downstairs to the vending machines and purchased a bottle of coke, and then began shaking it to make the bubbles disappear.

"Here, drink this," I said, handing him the drink. "My grandma and parents always used to give me flat Coke to help a bad stomach." I slid my back down the door and sat on the floor, feeling exhausted. I could have nodded off there and then, but I didn't––I would have been woken by his violent hurls anyway. Besides, I was worried about him.

I looked at my phone, which I'd used to navigate the hostel without turning on the lights.

Two and a half hours until we leave for Wat Rong Khun.

There were only two things that could sort this type of exhaustion––sleep or coffee. It wasn't worth going back to bed, not when I would need to be ready in an hour or so, so I resorted to my roots. The thing that got me through all those late nights and early mornings as a solicitor. Coffee, and lots of it.

Once Austin stopped gagging, I took him back to the comfort of his bed as he still clung onto his stomach.

"Wat Rong Khun, Wat Rong Khun, what's wrong, hun?"

I tried my best to be quiet but it seemed like the girls were up, as they all chanted in harmony. I'd had it the whole journey from Laos back into Thailand.

If you can't beat them, join them.

"Wat Rong Khun..." I sang as I gathered my things, making my way out of the room and closer to savouring the taste of that delicious coffee.

I must have sat in a daze as the smooth coffee took me into some sort of sweet abyss. It was either that or I'd fallen asleep while drinking it, because the girls were rushing past me like it was time to travel to the temple.

"Fleur, come on, the taxi is waiting," Paige said as she rushed out the door.

"Where's Austin?"

"He's not coming. He's too sick," she yelled back. I would have checked on him, but the taxi was waiting so I picked up my rucksack, placed it over my shoulder and sipped the remnants of the cold coffee that sat at the bottom of my cup.

"Package for Fleur," I overheard a young man say at the front desk.

"That's me, that's me," I bellowed enthusiastically. I'd not received a package like this off Austin for a while now. He was clearly making up to me the fact that he wasn't coming today. He was so thoughtful.

I tore open the package without hesitation and looked at the most beautiful tulip, bright yellow in colour, with a note tied to its stem.

Have you worked it out yet? If not, I'm sure this flower will jog your memory. I hope we get to see each other again soon x

Chapter Twenty

I didn't know whether to be disappointed or happy. I didn't know whether to launch the flower across the room in anger or to sob so deeply it would make the flower flourish and bloom.

I didn't know how to feel, my mind running away with itself as I stood still. Motionless.

"Fleur, come on!" Keira yelled loudly from outside, so I stuffed the tulip and note in my bag, not caring about the flower's integrity, and ran outside to get in the taxi.

I sat in silence as the girls continued to repeat Wat Rong Khun on the way to the temple. If only they knew what was wrong.

Levi had been sending me the flowers all along and this flower proved that. It was written in black ink. I saw it with my own eyes. And if this was the case, and I was ninety-nine percent sure of that, it meant Austin had been lying to me.

The butterflies in my stomach that should have been fluttering at the thought of Levi sending me such beautiful gestures during my travels had turned black. They were now laced with lies and deceit.

I wanted answers. I wanted to know why Austin, someone I'd considered to be my best friend, had lied to me. I wanted to know why I had messaged Levi and he hadn't responded, especially as he was sending me these flowers. But, as I drove away from Austin and the hostel towards the temple, I knew I'd have to wait for them. I knew I'd have to stew with my feelings and try to enjoy myself one last time with the girls before heading to Bangkok, and for the first time, I was thankful I wouldn't be continuing my travels with Austin.

I walked through the entrance, arm in arm with Paige, down a narrow bridge that crossed over a sea of carved arms and hands that seemed to reach out from the deepest parts of Hell. I took a few snaps on my camera, knowing I wouldn't be able to inside the temples. The all white exterior of the temples had me squinting as I walked around looking at the art-deco sculptures, some of which were recognizable as cartoon characters and video games.

"You don't seem yourself. Wat Rong Khun?" Paige asked, seeming really pleased with herself.

"Nothing, I'm fine. Just taking it all in," I said, trying to avoid eye contact.

"Don't lie to me. Don't make me ask you again."

I looked at her, trying to fight back tears of anger and hurt.

"Austin told me that he liked me and has done so from the moment he first saw me..."

"Oh, tell me something I don't know." Paige laughed.

"Well, he also told me he has been sending me flowers this whole time. And it made sense, because after he told me, the flowers stopped coming, until this morning. I got another flower. A tulip. And I know for certain it's not from Austin. I know deep down in my heart that it is from Levi, that gorgeous hunk I told you about––the one I had that fling with while I was visiting The Netherlands."

"I wondered why you hadn't been receiving any

flowers. I thought you were hiding them away from us because we'd been annoying you," Paige said with a naive tone. That was far from the truth.

"Absolutely not," I said, and began pacing as my mind started to connect more of the dots, like I was in court and about to deliver my closing argument. "The last flower I received was in Vietnam while we were in Hoan Kiem Lake. It was a lotus flower, the national flower of Vietnam, and it had a note that said *the perfect flower to sum up last night together*. I think he genuinely did get me that flower. It was even wrapped in different packaging, but I honestly think he's been hiding all the other flowers. I think that if he wasn't so ill this morning, I wouldn't have got this beautiful tulip and I would have been none the wiser." I pulled the tulip and note from my bag to show Paige.

"What a creep! And, that would explain why he always rushes into the hotels before us and normally wakes up at the crack of dawn." I nodded in disbelief, because it all made sense and I didn't want it to.

"I didn't even think about that. I honestly don't know whether to laugh or cry at this point. I thought he was my friend." I slumped myself down on a decorative bench, unsure whether I was allowed to sit on it as tourists tried to admire it around me.

"I thought he was our friend, too. This goes against everything our penis pact stands for," Paige said, nudging me, trying her best to make me laugh and she was successful. I couldn't not smile at her. How was it that as a grown woman I relied so much on a young adult to console me?

"I didn't realise we had rules in our gang. You could do with running over them for me so I don't break any of them."

"There's only one rule. Don't be a dick––we have enough of them on our wrists." The statement had me laughing from a pit deep inside my stomach. "What? It's a real rule, and Austin's behaviour violates our sacred penis laws."

"Stop! I'm laughing so much I'm gonna be sick," I said in between breaths and laughter.

"Okay, but just wait until Kiera and Courtney find out about this. They will be fuming."

"It's probably best if you don't tell them. I want to speak to Austin and get to the bottom of what's happened. I don't want this to ruin the final few days of this trip. I don't want it to be awkward." The last thing I wanted was for them to fall out with Austin. He'd become a big part of our lives––my life––and I held the fondest of memories, like how he'd bought me twenty-seven postcards and kept me safe. I was disappointed, but I wasn't about to start an Austin boycott, despite Paige encouraging it. She even mentioned a penis-pact murder. I was able to get on board with a lot of things the girls mentioned. I loved trying new things; I'd even got a tattoo, but I wasn't able to get on board with murdering Austin.

"Why not? It would be so cute. We'd be like Desperate Housewives!"

Oh, Paige.

After momentarily allowing myself to let go of the hurt, I immersed myself completely in the surroundings of Wat Rong Khun and all its beauty. I pulled up my big girl panties and put on a brave face in front of Kiera and Courtney, because I had to be okay––for them.

We arrived back at the hostel and went straight upstairs to check on Austin. He seemed to be feeling a little better, but he still looked horrendous. I couldn't help but feel a little smug about that.

"How was the temple? I'm so gutted I didn't come," Austin said. I perched myself on the edge of the bed while the other girls responded to him, remaining mute.

After a while, I glanced at Paige, signalling that I needed to talk to Austin. Straight away, she took it upon herself to distract the girls with nothing other than the possibility of getting another tattoo. Genius.

"You're quiet," Austin stated as he made himself more comfortable, propping his head up a little further in bed.

"Those flowers you were sending," I said as I watched his body turn rigid. I didn't bother beating around the bush, but I did want to give him a chance to confess. Him doing so would restore at least some of the respect I once held for him. "You didn't send them, did you?"

"I sent one of them," he smiled with sincerity and a little regret.

"Why did you do it? Why did you lie and pretend it was you all along?"

"Love made me do it, and sometimes love makes you do crazy things. Surely you can understand that?"

Love did make people do crazy things––things I'd seen a lot of in my line of work––things like taking children from their homes, but that was different. The one good thing I could say about Steve Palmer was that he loved his children. He'd acted out of love. Austin had acted out of nothing other than jealousy.

"I understand that you were jealous that someone else had my attention, but you had no reason to be.

What did you do with all the other packages? I assume there were more since I received one this morning?"

"I got rid of them."

I look at him bewilderingly. "Did you open them?"

"No, I promise. I wouldn't open your post. Fleur, please forgive me. I love you," he pleaded, knelt on his bed.

"I'm really pleased your morals were still intact when deciding whether or not to open my parcels, which you'd later throw away," I hissed, my tongue sharp and my tone sarcastic. I turned away, ready to pack my things, but anger bubbled inside me and I turned back to him. "The worst thing is, if you'd been honest about your feelings from the start, without the *fake* grand gesture, who knows? Maybe we could have been something more than friends in the future. Now, I'm not even sure our friendship will make it through this."

"Fleur, wait." Austin jumped up from his bed. "Maybe we can't be together, and that's okay, but please don't be the reason we don't have the best finale to our trip together. The others don't deserve that."

"Don't worry. I won't," I said and then found more of my voice. "I'm not going to be the reason. You are. They don't deserve it, which is why I won't be staying in Thailand for much longer with you guys.

I'm going back to The Netherlands, and you can explain to the girls why that's the case."

I gathered my things and walked out of the room with my head held high––as high as it had ever been held and this time, I wasn't going to let it fall.

Chapter
Twenty-One

"I thought you had a hotel booked for a week in Thailand. Please don't go. It isn't awkward," Keira said, clinging on to Courtney in devastation. I was the first of the group to be leaving, and I was pretty upset about it, too. Austin had spoken to the girls after our conversation, and said he'd leave instead of me because it was his fault. I admired him for that but the thing was, I wasn't leaving because of him. I couldn't wait a moment longer to speak to Levi, and seeing as he wasn't answering my calls or texts, I had to go in person. So, I was going to fly nearly halfway around the world to see him. Austin was right. Love really does make you do crazy things.

"I know it isn't but I have something I need to do in The Netherlands. Just because I'm going early, it doesn't mean I don't love you all. I've learnt so much from each of you, including the true meaning and value of friendship, something I hadn't experienced until I met you."

I looked at Keira and gave her a hug. "I mean, your infectious laugh and personality have shown me that it's okay to be a little reckless at times. Life is so much better when you're laughing." I glanced down at the penis tattoo on my wrist with a smile. "And Courtney, no matter what I'm going through in life, I know you'd come running right to my side, just like you do every day for Keira. You guys make the most beautiful couple." I sniffled, trying to hold back my tears.

"If you really have to go now, just come and meet us when you're done. Paige has convinced us to extend our trip and we're going to her neck of the woods," Keira said, with Courtney chirping in.

"Yeah, it will be the second time Keira's been down under in a very short space of time."

We all looked at Courtney and paused for a second before bursting into fits of laughter. Keira was infecting all of us with her vulgar mind, and Courtney was absolute proof of that.

"Paige, I see a lot of myself in you. You are the young woman I wished I could have been all those years ago and more. Strong, independent and living your life the way you want to live it. I know you'll never let anyone dim your light."

"Alright, grandma. Stop it otherwise you'll make me cry," Paige said with tissues at the ready.

"And Austin." I grabbed him by his arms and turned away from the girls, speaking quietly. "You've allowed me to realise the kind of woman I am and what I want out of a man. Thank you for all our memories. Despite everything, I think you're a good guy." I opened the taxi door and was about to get in, until Austin spoke. His voice was wavy and broken as he battled emotion.

"Wait! You've shown us things, too. Especially me." He swallowed the lump in his throat. "I was a knob. You go on about how you wanted to change and find yourself, but what you don't realise is you are pretty fantastic just the way you are. You've not really changed at all. You have been you the whole time and we have all fallen in love with you. Our trip would have been really different without you."

"You've shown me that even when you're in your thirties, you can still have a good time." Paige smirked, holding on to Austin's hand. She was doing her best to forgive him as I had, and I appreciated that. I knew she wouldn't forget about it, though, and neither would I. That was the Scorpio in us.

"You guys are awesome. I'm going to miss you all so much. You all have my number so stay in touch, okay?" I said as I slid into the taxi.

"We will. Love you, Fleur!" The girls somehow screamed in harmony as my taxi began moving towards the airport and towards all the answers I needed.

"Love you all so much more."

Those butterflies that had once been black had started to regain their colour. They were taking flight and began fluttering around my stomach as I sat on what seemed to be the longest flight I'd ever been on. I couldn't scroll on my phone mindlessly or keep trying to get hold of Levi, not with Airplane mode activated. I couldn't play any calming games or listen to music for very long, otherwise it would have no charge left when I arrived, and I needed it in case there was an emergency. All I could do was think, worry even, about what would happen next.

I didn't know what I'd say when I saw him.

Oh hello, Levi, it's me, Fleur, the crazy emotional lady you once slept with and who made off very quickly the following day. Don't suppose you've been sending me flowers, have you?

What idiot chooses to send flowers instead of texting or calling? Or am I the idiot who's plotted something so far from the truth?

I must have played out about twelve different scenarios like some sort of crazy person.

I didn't know what I'd do, never mind what he'd do. Would we run into each other's arms like in the movies? Or wrestle each other to the ground, kissing romantically. I hoped we would.

What if he isn't at home?

A rush of panic filled me at the thought of being sat outside his front door with enough tears to water his field of tulips. I didn't have a place to stay, but I knew about a few hostels in the area that I hoped would have room for a last minute traveller. Staying in a hostel again wouldn't be the worst thing in the world––I'd had lots of practice the month prior.

All I did know was that I needed to see him in person to know for sure––to hear why he was sending the flowers, to know why he hadn't texted or called me back and to ascertain if there was something between us.

Finally, I did manage to get some sleep on the plane, because after worrying for more than half the journey, there was nothing left other than to shut my eyes and have hope that Levi wouldn't see me as a crazy, stalker-like, damsel in distress.

"Where to, miss?" the taxi driver asked as he looked through his rear-view mirror. I caught a glimpse of myself, flustered and red. I wasn't spontaneous. I was a planner. Right down to the last detail––my travel journal was evidence of that––and I was straying from my itinerary. Nowhere did it say to book a last minute flight back to The Netherlands. Not once did it mention going to scout out a stranger, because that's what Levi was. A sexy, mysterious stranger.

"I don't actually know," I exclaimed with a look of madness. "Look, just drive towards this address. It's somewhere on the way, I think." I pointed at the map on my phone to a road I remembered walking along.

We began driving and edged closer towards the fields of...

Nothing.

Everywhere looked so different. Of course it did. It was June, and those gorgeous fields of tulips were long gone, with the only colour from the naturally growing plants on the embankments of the roads.

"There he is," I muttered and then quickly shouted, "Stop the car."

He was sitting on a tractor, which pulled along a huge machine that drove over the lines in the field and moved the soil underneath, creating room for a bulb to be dropped in and covered back up. The machinery was something I knew my grandparents would have sought after and would have saved their aching backs from having to plant the bulbs by hand.

I climbed out of the taxi and slammed the door. He didn't hear me. He couldn't hear anything over the grumbles of the tractor as it carried him away from his house and up the field.

I had to get closer.

"Levi," I yelled at the top of my voice, but nothing. No response. I must have bellowed his name ten times, and the more my voice cracked, letting out high pitch squeals in frustration. Frustration that I'd just flown thousands of miles and he couldn't hear me––couldn't see me.

My feet struggled to find balance on the uneven ground as I ran alongside his tractor, panting and out of breath from shouting his name. I could barely hear myself think as the tractor hissed and groaned and began to slow.

He'd seen me.

I looked at him as he gazed at me, his smile beaming from ear to ear. He watched me as I moved in front of his tractor, which had now come to a stop. I stood in front of it, dripping with sweat as a heat wave, somehow hotter than the weather I'd experienced in South East Asia, swept the country.

With one muscular arm holding onto the roof of the tractor, he lowered himself to the ground. Damn, he was so hot. I could have drooled at the sight. It was as hot as Captain America holding on to a helicopter, something I'd not understood the buzz about until I saw the movie.

His smile gradually faded as it took note of my pointed eyebrows, standing in front of his tractor like some sort of raging protestor.

"I guess you didn't like the flowers?" he said casually, one arm resting on the side of his tractor.

"Like them? Like them?" I said, stumbling through my words. It was him. I knew it. "I loved them, Levi, but why the hell have you not messaged me back? I've had to fly all the way from goddamn Thailand. Do you not use your phone?" I remained still, as he slowly edged towards me.

"What do you mean?" He pulled out his phone with a look of confusion.

"I have texted and called you so many times, but you never messaged back." I also took my phone out of my bag so I could show him.

We were inches apart and his scent was the same, making my nose tingle and butterflies flutter more than they ever had.

"I've received no texts. Let me see." He took my phone off me, swiping and tapping frantically. "You've been messaging the wrong number. That seven should be a one."

"What?" I gasped, and placed my hands on my face like some sort of Macaulay Culkin impersonation. I then pulled out my journal, feeling as small as I could as I read the number as I should have. "Oh my god. I'm so sorry."

Levi grabbed my arm as I started to freak out. His touch sent shivers down my spine and instantly pulled me from a state of panic.

"It's fine, Fleur. You're here now. That's all that matters." His voice was deep yet the low hum soothed me. I could feel his force as he pulled me into him, as close as we could get. So close I could feel the rough material of his pants against my bare legs and his breath against my neck as he spoke gently into my ear. "I can't believe we've spent the past minute or so talking about our phones instead of fucking in this field. Right here. Right now." His words had me flustered, and then feeling his excitement push up against me made me want to tear off his clothes.

Our mouths met, sending me into paradise where only he and I existed. The heat radiated against us and got way too much. Standing outside, unshaded and entirely vulnerable to each other, we took our retreat inside to his room.

Chapter Twenty-Two

I awoke in a familiar place––a bedroom with whites and greys sitting under cottage-like beams that ran across the ceiling. However, this time I wasn't alone.

"Hey, beautiful. Good sleep?" Levi kissed my forehead as I nestled into his arm.

"Incredible," I said with an inhale, then released a deep, contented sigh. If I'd had the option to stay in that position forever, I'd have taken it.

"Good. I'd offer to make you food but I don't

want to scare you off like last time." He playfully nudged me with a huge grin plastered on his face.

"Oh, don't worry. I'm not going anywhere. You might end up ghosting me again." I smirked at him.

"Right. That's it." In an instant, I was pulled underneath the covers, being pushed closer and closer to that moment of release while drowning in the whites of the linen. I was in heaven.

Nobody pinch me.

Fresh air caressed my face as I pulled off the duvet, sweat dripping down my brow as I recovered from multiple moments of pleasure.

"Wow. That's never happened before," I said, still breathless and quaking from his touch.

"One of my many talents." He appeared from under the cover and then hopped out of bed. His broad figure shadowed over me, and I scanned his body as he stood bare and exposed but with as much confidence as the day I'd met him. "Come on, I'll make you some food, and you can tell me all about your travels."

I had a lot to tell––tales of lies, deceit, reckless-ness, friendship and of lands so beautiful. I'd barely seen half of what I wanted to see across the globe, and the impromptu stop in The Netherlands was delaying my travels, but I didn't feel held back. This time, work wasn't a priority and Connor wasn't building hopes of us travelling together. I was here on my terms.

I cringed as I told Levi about Austin. How he'd lied about him sending me the flowers. How he'd even disposed of some of the packages that Levi had sent. I could tell Levi was irritated. His expression told me that as he bit his tongue. I hopped up from my chair and wrapped my arms around his bare torso as he cooked us breakfast. After the long flight, a peaceful sleep and even more time in between the sheets, I'd lost all track of time, and breakfast seemed like the most appropriate meal.

"I'm so happy it was you sending me the flowers. I'm glad he didn't get rid of that final flower, other-wise, how could I have been sure with your cryptic messages?" I said, my lips pressing against his back, soothing the scratches I'd placed there only minutes before as he'd rocked my world.

"How many more people would have been sending you them?" he asked with a small laugh.

I began jokingly counting on my fingers and with each addition I was given a sly look.

"Touché, Miss Fleur." He opened a draw in the kitchen that had loose papers in and pulled out the only stack that was paperclipped together, handing it to me. "I hope that seeing these will make you forget about these countless men of yours."

I flicked through the pieces of paper, each one an invoice from a different florist––florists in South East Asia. Some were business invoices, but the majority were just email trails confirming the quote Levi had asked for them to write. I scanned the pages, some of which made images of beautiful flowers and beautifully hand written notes I'd received appear in my mind. Reminders of the rose, lily, daisy and lavender, but no mention of the lotus that Austin sent in order to make the gesture appear to be his. Other pages were not as familiar and disclosed the flowers and notes I would have received. My eyes caught two in particular.

An orchid to many is a symbol of strength, love and beauty. It doesn't have anything on you, Fleur x

There is a miracle waiting to happen and if you look for it, you'll see magic along the way x

The second note, which was meant to arrive with a blush pink peony, made goosebumps rise on my forearms and enhanced that fuzzy feeling I felt just thinking about Levi.

"Is it a miracle that we found each other? Would you really class that as miraculous?" I looked up to him with the widest of eyes as he sat down next to me, held my hand in both of his and gently pressed his lips against it.

"Do you not think it's extraordinary that you came all this way to see me? My number was in your book and you tried to get in touch but could not. Then, that idiotic man-child you told me of hid the flowers I'd sent you, and yet, you still somehow found your way back to me. I'd say my luck has turned. I'd say it was a miracle. You are my miracle."

The ground outside was bare yet my heart flourished like a tulip in spring as his voice caressed me with his magical words. With his touch. His love.

I'd learnt a lot while travelling. I'd learnt I couldn't run away from my problems, because they'd find me again, and if they didn't, other problems would.

I'd learnt I was going to make mistakes, some as small as Pluto and others the size of Jupiter, and that was okay, too. Just like on occasion, my gut was going to be wrong about things, too. All of this allowed me to grow as a person because I could learn from them.

I'd always seen myself as a perfect solicitor, when truthfully, I was far from perfect. Was that a bad thing? No, it wasn't, no matter how many people told me otherwise. I was good at my job, excellent even, and I knew that was down to having a whole lot of emotion that made me see things differently. I wasn't a robot, nor did I have a corporate face that I could switch on and off when I needed to, because I was only human. A coffee drinking, mistake making, heart on both my sleeves wearing, penis pact making, human––and gosh, that felt so good.

"I best check on the food," Levi said as he was about to get back up from his seat and continue making my food. I stopped him in his tracks with a kiss, and then captured a few pictures of us both. One picture captured us looking lovingly into each other's eyes, one pictured as the cutest couple, and a final picture caught me eyeing up his torso. *Busted.*

I then sat back down and waited as patiently as I could. I forwarded the pictures to the penis pact group chat and just seconds later was spammed with responses.

"Oh my god, look at those pecs!"

"Hubba hubba, you sexy pair."

"Fleur, you look so happy." I opened the picture once more and noticed how serene I looked, wearing a sincere smile. I *was* happy, and with the smile still gracing my face, I knew it was because I was content with my life. I'd found myself.

I'd found parts of myself while I travelled and in my newest friends––my best friends. I'd even discovered parts of myself I'd hidden for so long in order to please my parents, when all along they'd been rooting for me no matter what. And then there was Levi. I'd not known him for long, but he was already bringing out the right side of me––the best side. I knew whatever journey we were to go on would be right for me, because the biggest thing I'd learnt was that I didn't have to conform to a man––boyfriend or husband, boss or colleague and even a stranger walking down the street—because I was enough and I was able to live life on my own terms.

"Madam, your wentelteefjes are ready." He placed the native dish in front of me, which was basically fancy French toast, and the smell transported me back to a simpler time. A time when I'd watched my grandparents in the fields. A time when I was also happy and content with being me. And for the first time in forever, I was perfectly fine with being in the here and now, because I was happier than that little girl playing in a field full of flowers.

Epilogue

Six months later...

"Are you sure you aren't allowed in?" Andrea asked, holding onto my hand. I could feel it shaking with nerves as the clock approached ten in the morning, the time she was due in court.

"I can't. Family proceedings are private matters. No public allowed and I'm not representing you. Besides, you're in safe hands with Olly. He'll look after you." Olly nodded in thanks and started to usher

Andrea towards the door. "But, I'll be right here with Levi."

Time had passed us both by in the blink of an eye. What had been months of travelling the world together seemed like days. We'd gone from zero to one hundred in the matter of a few weeks. I'd barely left his house. One minute we couldn't bear to leave the bedroom, the next minute he was hiring people to tend to his house and garden while we ran away together.

We went through countless interviews to find the right person because his tulip fields held so many memories of his late wife. It turned out he was also being held back, because he'd always wanted to travel, too, but it hadn't been a person holding him back. It was his tulip fields.

Then, after a week or so of showing them the ropes, we were on a plane excited to start our travels, with the first destination being New Zealand. I was never going to pass up an opportunity to see the girls again, and Paige was the perfect host. She acted as our very own tour guide, showing us the best places to drink, eat and pull guys. Thankfully, I didn't have to worry about the latter. I had Levi, but Paige pulled enough men for the both of us.

We then did a tour of the USA, starting with the sights of the Golden Gate Bridge and finishing with the bright lights of The Big Apple, without forgetting a short stay at a romantic resort in Hawaii on the way. I always had the best ideas, until Levi had the idea that when we finished travelling, I should move back to The Netherlands and move in with him.

God damn, Dutch hunk, always doing one better.

Of course I said yes. A couple of years ago I'd contemplated moving back to The Netherlands, but my relationship with Connor had just been starting and I didn't want to have to learn a new judicial system. Years on, I welcomed the change and challenge, and applied for the Qualified Lawyers Transfer Scheme, an assessment that would allow me to be a dual-qualified lawyer practising both UK and Dutch Law.

I adjusted my head as it rested on Levi's shoulder. I'd flinch each time the sound of a door opening filled the hall, eagerly awaiting the outcome for Andrea and her children. She'd spent the past months having minimal contact with her children, fighting to have joint custody with her soon to be ex-husband, who claimed that Andrea couldn't provide for her children without his help. What was it with certain men thinking that women couldn't survive without them?

Andrea had been a shell of herself all those months ago when I'd first met her, and after seeing her prepare for court, I knew that now. She was nervous, but stood tall and strong. She was scared for her children, but she never stopped fighting for them. She was tired, but that didn't stop her from getting a full time job and working through the exhaustion to prove to the judge her commitment to the children.

With Steve, Andrea was a flame that was constantly being smothered, not allowed to burn at her brightest. I could see that, and I knew for certain that my gut wasn't wrong about them. I hoped that the judge would see through Steve.

The courtroom door opened and out stormed an upset Steve, with a familiar looking solicitor standing behind him. Samuel was posh and proper but couldn't drink a spirit straight to save his life. Olly shouldn't have been worried and I did chuckle to myself knowing that he was the person who replaced me. I felt sorry for Janine.

Steve was about to head out until he spotted me and stopped in his tracks.

"This is all your fault," he said, with a poisonous tongue about to launch his attack. "You whispered in her ear and gave her an inflated sense of confidence. Truth is, she's nothing more than scum." His solicitor tried to control his behaviour with a swift tug on his shirt, but he pulled himself away and glared at me.

"Why, Mr Palmer. Andrea is an extraordinary woman––not just for raising her two beautiful children or for getting a well paid job, but for putting up with you for all those years. I personally don't believe I had any impact on Andrea other than being a friend for her in her time of need. I do believe that she saw something so awful, so terrible in you, that ever since she has strived to become an even better version of herself because she couldn't bear to be anything like you." I stood with my shoulders high and my eyes glued to his. Not once did I look down or break eye contact.

"You bitch," he muttered, loud enough for his solicitor and Levi to jump into action. He towered over Steve despite standing behind me. He just stood there, as a warning, but he didn't try to fight my battle for me because he knew I was capable of winning them all. He was my protector, and that's all I'd ever wanted in a man.

"That's enough. Let's go." Samuel surprised me with his raised voice as he ordered Steve to step away.

"I'm so glad I finally got to see the true side of Mr Steven Palmer. I'm sure everyone else will get to, as well," I said as Steve walked away and Andrea came bursting out of the door, beaming with joy despite catching the latter end of the conversation.

"What was that about? What did he say to you?"

"Andrea, you have nothing to worry about. Fleur kicked his arse," Levi said quickly, and held my hand as though he was proud of me. Heck, I was proud of myself.

"Well, I had no doubt about that." Andrea smiled

"So, what was the outcome? By the look of Steve I'm guessing we got a good one?"

"The children will reside with me. Steve will have them over the weekends but that will change if he tries to take my children away from me again."

"That's absolutely amazing. Congratulations, Andrea." I wrapped my arms around her, no longer feeling her vulnerability, but the strength she held internally.

"Yep, and we're going for full custody after the divorce. I'm sure in that time we'll be able to build up a pretty good case against him."

"I knew you were the guy for the job," I said to Olly as I held my hand out.

"Thank you, Fleur." He shook my hand with a firm grip and leant into me. "Are you sure I can't persuade you to come over to the dark side and work for our firm? We could use a decent lawyer like you."

"That's very kind, but I'm moving to The Nether-lands and I don't think they'd pay my travel expenses every time I needed to travel to court." I laughed a little.

"You're probably right." Olly turned his head and then turned back. "I never told you this, but I've always been a little intimidated by you. I hated that you were going to be a better solicitor than me."

"Oh, I know. Maybe one day you will be. Can I give you a tip?"

"Always," he said, leaning in to hear all my secrets. To gain all my wisdom.

"The best solicitors have empathy, and lots of it. You'll do well to connect to your clients instead of separating yourself from them. My secret is that I care." He paused for a second and then nodded.

"You do, don't you? Good to see you again, Fleur."

I shook Olly's hand and looked at Andrea. I could almost see a bright light emitting from her smile as it beamed from one side of the court to the other.

"Right, we best head to the house, but we'll see you tonight for celebratory drinks before we catch our flight."

"I can't wait. Thank you again. Not just for being here today but for taking me in when I needed someone and I had no one to rely on. You may not have represented me, but you practically saved my life and you gave me all the hope I'd ever need to get my children back. I'll be forever grateful to you, Fleur," Andrea said.

Levi and I left the court and made our way to my house, but not before I wiped away more tears and held onto Andrea for what seemed like an eternity.

At first, the thought of moving to The Netherlands had my nerves on high alert, until I realised they were just that. Nerves--worry masking the excitement I was feeling deep down, all because my head was tuned to believe something would go wrong, but I had no reason to be in that frame of mind. Levi had given me no reason to think it would. In fact, he'd shared nothing but love with me. He hadn't proposed but that was okay. Moving in with him was a big enough step, maybe even the biggest. The thought of spending the rest of my life with him was probably the best feeling in the world, and I should have known. I'd seen most of it with him.

I shut my eyes as I closed the door to my house in London for the last time, ready to give the keys to the estate agent.

"Ready to go, or do you need a minute?" Levi asked, taking my hand in his.

"No, I'm okay. I'm ready." I smiled with tears glistening in my eyes.

"I love you, Fleur."

"Ik hou ook van jou, Levi." I squeezed his hand as I walked down the few steps away from one of the only homes I'd even known, knowing that I was returning to the only other place I knew I'd call my home.

When my parents had found out I'd be moving to The Netherlands, they'd made the decision to sell the house. I couldn't quite believe that London would no longer be our family home, but as I wiped the tears from my eyes, Levi reminded me there would be plenty of opportunities to return. Janine and Andrea still lived there, and they wouldn't forgive me if I abandoned them. That wasn't me anymore. I knew that.

I pulled out my new journal, containing all the things we wanted to do together in the next year––my first year back in The Netherlands, and with Christmas just around the corner, I couldn't wait to document the perfect Christmas with him. And it would be perfect, because we'd made the journal together.

"So, what next?"

Sneak Peek of
worth
lying
for
by K J Ellis

Keeley

I've never been the type of person to bite my tongue when I feel strongly about something, or if I disagree with what a person might say or do.

That applies to my brother's best friend, Drake. God, he gets under my skin like a bad fucking smell. He's a pig-headed player and I swear he gets a thrill out of winding me up——something he does a lot.

Whenever he's in the same room as me——it doesn't matter who's there——he throws digs at me or finds some way to embarrass me.

He has no filter. Either that or he just doesn't care

about what he says or whether or not he's hurt my feelings. Which is what he does the majority of time. I doubt he would care anyway.

I should have learnt by now that the more I react the more he continues to torment me, but I can't help myself.

I'm mouthy and don't take no shit—most of the time.

I give as good as I get, don't get me wrong but it doesn't matter if I stay quiet or have it out with him, he only does it more.

It must be how he gets his kicks when there isn't a woman on top of him——or underneath him——to keep him occupied.

What makes matters worse... Drake happens to be hot as hell. He has a body chiselled from stone, and a smile that could melt your undies off. I find it hard to stop myself from throwing myself at him and let him do wicked, dirty things to me.

I've heard the stories about Drake and this sexual encounters. I can't not, when every girl he's slept with likes to brag about it. It makes me sick when I hear the way girls talk about him. It's not something they should be proud of. Drake sleeps with anyone who has a pair of tits and spreads their legs so eagerly and gives him exactly what he wants.

Sex.

Nothing more, nothing less.

Apparently, he makes that abundantly clear before-hand, or so I've heard.

Then jealousy would take over. I just couldn't win where Drake was concerned.

I hate him with a passion, yet I lust over him like a moth to a flame. I'm fucking drawn to that fucker whether I like it or not.

I fight with him, but I wanna have his hands all over me. I hate him, yet I wanna be the girl to tame him. The only girl.

How is that even possible?

I must have a screw loose for thinking these things. Not only that, my brother would kill me if he ever found out I was lusting over Drake. He's been best friends with my brother since the day they both started kindergarten and the fact I'm eight years younger wouldn't sit well with Arlo.

But the heart wants, what it wants.

I'm screwed regardless.

Acknowledgments

POV: Your acknowledgements are longer than the actual book. Just kidding, although it's close! Where do I start?

To you, my reader. Thank you for picking up this book and for taking a chance on me. You guys keep me going on the odd occasion I don't want to and I can't thank you enough for that.

To my A-Tribe. You all get me through general life, never mind the amount you cheer me on:

Heather, my incredible editor & my Pepsi-Max loving, snack consuming, cuddle giving friend. You swooped in and edited this book like a superhero and I'll love you forever for all the support you give me.

Eleanor, my insanely talented cover designer. You get me through thick and thin, giving me the best tools to promote my books, but you also kick me up the arse when I doubt myself. You rock and I love you!

Lizzie, our series organiser and one hell of a force of nature! Thank you for keeping us all in check and for promoting this series. P.S. you really do have the loveliest carrots...

And to Riah, Jessop and Rossi. You guys keep me going with your love and support. Truth is, I don't know what I'd do without any of you!

To my alpha & beta readers. You have been by my side since I started to write this book, some of you even before! Thank you for your love and honesty. You guys help me better myself and I'm so lucky to have you. A special thanks to Emma for all the hours you gave up, for all the messages kicking me into shape—thank you. I probably wouldn't have finished this book without you.

To my NWAA crew. I want you to know that your love and support goes a really long way, not just in my writing but also in my day job. Thank you for being the #OneCrew I can rely on.

To Abi, one incredible friend and an inspiration in more aspects than one. Thank you for being there in life, but also in helping me research the journey Fleur embarks on. She wouldn't have got as far around the world if it hadn't been for you.

To Evan, for inspiring me every day. For your advice, your spark of imagination and for all the motivation you give me. Thank you. Who knows? Maybe one day I'll convince you to write your own book.

To everyone else I may not have mentioned above —those who share my stories with their friends, those I've met at book signings, those who continue to like, share and review my books and everyone else who continues to impact my writing journey. It's for you I keep writing. Thank you for all you do, I see you all and it means the absolute world to me.

All my love,

D J Cook xx

Also by
D J Cook

The TLC Series

Tamsin

Liam

Printed in Great Britain
by Amazon

38965838R00139